WESTERN
ANIMAL HEROES

WESTERN ANIMAL HEROES

AN ANTHOLOGY OF STORIES

by

Ernest Thompson Seton

Compiled and Edited

by

Stephen Zimmer

SUNSTONE
PRESS

SANTA FE

Illustrations by Ernest Thompson Seton

Sunstone books may be purchased for educational, business, or sales promotional
use. For information please write: Special Markets Department, Sunstone Press,
P.O. Box 2321, Santa Fe, New Mexico 87504-2321.

Library of Congress Cataloging-in-Publication Data:

Seton, Ernest Thompson, 1860–1946.
   Western animal heroes: an anthology of stories / by Ernest Thompson
Seton; compiled and edited by Stephen Zimmer.
       p. cm.
   Includes bibliographical references.
   ISBN: 0-86534-475-2 (hardcover)   ISBN: 0-86534-356-X (softcover)
   1. Animals—West (U.S.)—anecdotes. I. Zimmer, stephen. II. Title.

QL791.S498 2005
591.978—dc22

                              2004030964

WWW.SUNSTONEPRESS.COM
SUNSTONE PRESS / POST OFFICE BOX 2321 / SANTA FE, NM 87504-2321 /USA
(505) 988-4418 / *ORDERS ONLY* (800) 243-5644 / FAX (505) 988-1025

Contents

Introduction

Ernest Thompson Seton

aturalist Ernest Thompson Seton was a leader of the wildlife conservation movement that developed in the United States in the early decades of the 20th Century. As a result of extensive study of wild animal behavior he became concerned about the loss of wildlife and its habitat and endeavored to enlighten the American public regarding its plight. Through lectures and magazine articles he stressed the importance of enacting conservation laws and establishing wildlife sanctuaries. He exerted an even greater influence as a champion of endangered wildlife by writing realistic animal stories that were popular in both the United States and Canada.

Born in 1860 in England, Seton moved with his family to Ontario, Canada six years later. During his early years there he developed a profound interest in the outdoors and its inhabitants. While his brothers spent hours at play, Seton tramped the woods surrounding his home and made notes about and drew pictures of the animals he observed.

After his family moved to Toronto in 1876, Seton chose to study art. He first entered an art apprenticeship in Toronto, which was followed by instruction at the Ontario School of Art. Animals were his primary subject. After completing training in Canada, he sailed to England for a year of study in London.

He returned to Canada in 1882 when he and his brother homesteaded land on the plains of western Manitoba. Whenever he had opportunity over the next few years he studied birds and their behavior in the field and made drawings of them. He compiled the results of his work in a scientific monograph titled, *Birds of Manitoba*, which was published in 1891. While in Manitoba, Seton received several commissions for wildlife illustrations, the most important of which was an assignment for a thousand drawings to illustrate *The Century Dictionary*.

By 1890 Seton decided that he was not destined to be a farmer and resolved to devote his full energy to the study and portrayal of wildlife through art. As a result he left the Canadian plains and made arrangements to study art in Paris, sailing there that year.

In between art studies in France during the next decade Seton traveled to the United States where he ventured West to observe animals. The first trip was the most important in terms of his subsequent career. In the fall of 1893 he went to the ranch country of northeastern New Mexico to trap wolves which resulted in the capture of the notorious wolf, Lobo. He later recounted the capture in story form and placed it as the lead story in his first book of illustrated animal stories, *Wild Animals I Have Known*. The overwhelming response to the book in the United States and Canada ultimately brought him national prominence as a writer, artist, and naturalist.

On later trips Seton found material in other wilderness areas of the West that he used to write more animal stories. The stories first appeared in popular magazines such as *Scribners'*, *Colliers*, and *Ladies Home Journal* and were later compiled in books such as *Lives of the Hunted*, *Animal Heroes*, and *Wild Animal Ways*.

Seton was in Paris in July of 1894 when he met a fellow American named Grace Gallatin. They married in May of 1896 in New York where they took up residence. Gallatin was also a writer and subsequently wrote two books, *A Woman Tenderfoot* (1900) and *Nimrod's Wife* (1907), that recounted adventures she experienced with her husband on their western trips.

Their first trip together was to Yellowstone Park in the summer of 1897. Afterward, they visited the Crow Indian Agency in Montana and then went to the dude ranch of Howard Eaton in the Dakota Badlands. A year later they returned to the Dakotas to visit Eaton and traveled from there to the Tetons of Wyoming and the Bitterroots of Idaho.

In the summer of 1899 Seton conducted a lecture tour in conjunction with the publication of *Wild Animals I Have Known*. With Grace by his side he traveled through western Canada lecturing as he went. Afterward they headed south to California and made a long stop in San Francisco which was followed by an excursion tour of the Sierra Nevadas. They returned to the East by way of the Grand Canyon in Arizona. Along the way he successfully gathered source material that he later used in a number of animal stories.

In conjunction with the study of natural history Seton became interested in Native American culture and ultimately became knowledgeable about many tribes. From his study, he believed that Indians lived symbiotically with the natural world and served as a model that modern Americans might emulate. He wrote extensively along that line, especially in his *The Book of Woodcraft and Indian Lore* which appeared in 1912.

In pursuing his interest in Native Americans, he developed a youth program in 1902 called the Woodcraft Indians that focused on the study of American Indian culture. The program was immediately popular with young people, and its success led Seton to become involved with the founding of the Boy Scouts of America in 1910. He wrote that organization's first handbook and served as its first Chief Scout.

Throughout this time Seton continued to write both animal stories and scholarly articles and books. In 1909 he published his most ambitious scientific work, *Life Histories of Northern Animals*, that recorded his discovery and study of fifty-nine species in Manitoba.

Although Seton's studies and drawings of animals had made him well known in the scientific community, he did not come to the notice of the American public at large until the 1898 publication of *Wild Animals I Have Known* which established the realistic animal story as a new literary form. The stories in the book were biographies of eight animals based on behavior that Seton either observed in the field or learned from people who had. At the same time he added fictional elements to some in order to dramatize the life story and heighten the tragedy of the animals's deaths.

Overall, his primary interest in his stories was to view each animal from its perspective, rather than from a human one. His "man against nature" concept had not been employed by any other American and Canadian nature writer of the time.

Seton stated the theme of the book in his introductory note:

"These stories are true. Although I have left the strict line of historical truth in many places, the animals in this book were all real characters. They lived the lives I have depicted, and showed the stamp of heroism and personality more strongly by far than it has been in the power of my pen to tell."

In keeping with Seton's view, the animals in his stories are heroic while the human characters, whether hunters, cowboys or trappers, are portrayed as undesirable types, if not outright villains. For example, the cowboys that appear as characters in "The Pacing Mustang" and "Tito" have a weakness for whiskey and for squandering their pay for good times with their fellows in town. They are pictured in much an opposite manner than the "noble knights of the range" prevalent in other western stories and books of the period.

Importantly, however, even though Seton was a "dude" from the East, he spent enough time in the West that he came to appreciate the best qualities of the cowboys and the manner in which they worked on the range. It is evident in his stories that he admired their skill in handling horses and cattle and ultimately their true character.

Because most of Seton's stories are about hunted animals, they invariably have tragic endings. In the "Note to the Reader," of *Wild Animals I Have Known*, he explained that "the fact that these stories are true is the reason why all are tragic. The life of a wild animal always has a tragic end." In the later volume, *Lives of the Hunted*, he added that "there is only one way to make an animal's history un-tragic, and that is to stop before the last chapter."

The stories herein are representative of the animal stories that Seton wrote from experiences on his western trips and are presented in chronological order relative to when Seton either observed or learned the story.

Stephen Zimmer
Cimarron, New Mexico

Lobo

The King of Currumpaw

While in Paris in November of 1891, Seton met a fellow American named Virginia Fitz-Randolph. They became close friends, and a year later sailed together to the United States. Upon arrival, Seton was invited to her parents' home in New Jersey.

In conversation with Fitz-Randolph's father Seton learned that he owned a cattle ranch in northeastern New Mexico and that the ranchers of the area had been suffering devastating wolf depredations on their herds. Knowing of Seton's knowledge of wolf behavior, Fitz-Randolph offered to pay the naturalist's expenses if he would go to the ranch and teach the cowboys how to eradicate some of the wolf population. For his effort Seton was to be allowed to redeem the hides of the trapped wolves for bounty money.

Seton agreed to the arrangement and left for New Mexico in the fall, arriving in Clayton on October 22, 1893. He wrote in his autobiography that when he stepped from the train, "My cash on hand was $80, supplied by Fitz-Randolph. Out of this, after paying

$18.31 for ammunition, $34.65 railway fare, $10.41 for sundries including meals, I had remaining $16.83 to return to him."

Seton stayed for a month on Fitz-Randolph's L Cross F Ranch southwest of Clayton. While working there, he trapped many coyotes but was unable to catch any wolves. In addition to traps, he also used poison in an attempt to kill wolves. He stopped the practice, however, after he learned that a cowboy on a neighboring ranch had died an agonizing death by mistakenly drinking wolf poison.

In January Seton moved his trapping operation northwest of Clayton to the Currumpaw River. From the local cowboys he learned that the surrounding range had been preyed upon for years by a particularly intelligent, yet treacherous cattle-killing wolf, known as Lobo (Spanish for wolf). It was the capture of that wolf and the subsequent recounting of the event that led Seton to financial success. The renowned conservationist Dr. William Hornaday wrote that Seton's story of Lobo was "the most wonderful true story of wild-animal cunning that has appeared in English so far."

The story was first published in *Scribner's Magazine* in November of 1894 as "The King of Currumpaw: A Wolf Story." It then became the lead story in Seton's first and most famous collection of animal stories, *Wild Animals I Have Known*. As an example of the book's popularity, it was reprinted ten times in its first two years of existence.

Lobo

The King of Currumpaw

I

urrumpaw is a vast cattle range in northern New Mexico. It is a land of rich pastures and teeming flocks and herds, a land of rolling mesas and precious running waters that at length unite in the Currumpaw River, from which the whole region is named. And the king whose despotic power was felt over its entire extent was an old gray wolf.

Old Lobo, or the king, as the Mexicans called him, was the gigantic leader of a remarkable pack of gray wolves, that had ravaged the Currumpaw Valley for a number of years. All the shepherds and ranchmen knew him well, and, whenever he appeared with his trusty band, terror reigned supreme among the cattle, and wrath and despair among their owners. Old Lobo was a

giant among wolves, and was cunning and strong in proportion to his size. His voice at night was well-known and easily distinguished from that of any of his fellows. An ordinary wolf might howl half the night about the herdsman's bivouac without attracting more than a passing notice, but when the deep roar of the old king came booming down the canon, the watcher bestirred himself and prepared to learn in the morning that fresh and serious inroads had been made among the herds.

Old Lobo's band was but a small one. This I never quite understood, for usually, when a wolf rises to the position and power that he had, he attracts a numerous following. It may be that he had as many as he desired, or perhaps his ferocious temper prevented the increase of his pack. Certain is it that Lobo had only five followers during the latter part of his reign. Each of these, however, was a wolf of renown, most of them were above the ordinary size, one in particular, the second in command, was a veritable giant, but even he was far below the leader in size and prowess. Several of the band, besides the two leaders, were especially noted. One of those was a beautiful white wolf, that the Mexicans called Blanca; this was supposed to be a female, possibly Lobo's mate. Another was a yellow wolf of remarkable swiftness, which, according to current stories had, on several occasions, captured an antelope for the pack.

It will be seen, then, that these wolves were thoroughly well-known to the cowboys and shepherds. They were frequently seen and oftener heard, and their lives were intimately associated with those of the cattlemen, who would so gladly have destroyed them. There was not a stockman on the Currumpaw who would not readily have given the value of many steers for the scalp of any one of Lobo's band, but they seemed to possess charmed lives, and defied all manner of devices to kill them. They scorned all hunters, derided all poisons, and continued, for at least five years, to exact their tribute from the Currumpaw ranchers to the extent, many said, of a cow each day. According to this estimate, therefore, the band had killed more than two thousand of the finest stock, for, as was only too well-known, they selected the best in every instance.

The old idea that a wolf was constantly in a starving state, and therefore ready to eat anything, was as far as possible from the truth in this case, for these freebooters were always sleek and well-conditioned, and were in fact most fastidious about what they ate. Any animal that had died from natural causes, or that was diseased or tainted, they would not touch, and they even rejected anything that had been killed by the stockman. Their choice and daily food was the tenderer part of a freshly killed yearling heifer. An old bull or cow they disdained, and though they occasionally took a young calf or colt, it was quite clear that veal or horseflesh was not their favorite diet. It was also known that they were not fond of mutton, although they often amused themselves by killing sheep. One night in November, 1893, Blanca and the yellow wolf killed two hundred and fifty sheep, apparently for the fun of it, and did not eat an ounce of their flesh.

These are examples of many stories which I might repeat, to show the ravages of this destructive band. Many new devices for their extinction were tried each year, but still they lived and throve in spite of all the efforts of their foes. A great price was set on Lobo's head, and in consequence poison in a score of subtle forms was put out for him, but he never failed to detect and avoid it. One thing only he feared—that was firearms, and knowing full well that all men in this region carried them, he never was known to attack or face a human being. Indeed, the set policy of his band was to take refuge in flight whenever, in the daytime, a man was descried, no matter at what distance. Lobo's habit of permitting the pack to eat only that which they themselves had killed was in numerous cases their salvation, and the keenness of his scent to detect the taint of human hands or the poison itself, completed their immunity.

On one occasion, one of the cowboys heard the too familiar rallying-cry of Old Lobo, and stealthily approaching, he found the Currumpaw pack in a hollow, where they had rounded up a small herd of cattle. Lobo sat apart on a knoll, while Blanca with the rest was endeavoring to cut out a young cow, which they had selected; but the cattle were standing in a compact mass with their heads outward, and presented to the foe a line of horns, unbroken save when some cow, frightened by a fresh onset of the wolves, tried to retreat into the middle of the herd. It was only by taking advantage of these breaks that the wolves had succeeded at all in wounding the selected cow, but she was far from being disabled, and it seemed that Lobo at length lost patience with his followers, for he left his position on the hill, and, uttering a deep roar, dashed toward the herd. The terrified rank broke at his charge, and he sprang in among them. Then the cattle scattered like the pieces of a bursting bomb. Away went the chosen victim, but ere she had gone twenty-five yards Lobo was upon her. Seizing her by the neck he suddenly held back with all his force and so threw her heavily to the ground. The shock must have been tremendous, for the heifer was thrown heels over head. Lobo also turned a somersault, but immediately recovered himself, and his followers falling on the poor cow, killed her in a few seconds. Lobo took no part in the killing—after having thrown the victim, he seemed

Lobo showing the pack how to kill beef.

to say, "Now, why could not some of you have done that at once without wasting so much time?"

The man now rode up shouting, the wolves as usual retired, and he, having a bottle of strychnine, quickly poisoned the carcass in three places, then went away, knowing they would return to feed, as they had killed the animal themselves. But next morning, on going to look for his expected victims, he found that, although the wolves had eaten the heifer, they had carefully cut out and thrown aside all those parts that had been poisoned.

The dread of this great wolf spread yearly among the ranchmen, and each year a larger price was set on his head, until at last it reached $1,000, an unparalleled wolf-bounty, surely; many a good man has been hunted down for less. Tempted by the promised reward, a Texan ranger named Tannerey came one day galloping up the canyon of the Currumpaw. He had a superb outfit for wolf-hunting—the best of guns and horses, and a pack of enormous wolf-hounds. Far out on the plains of the Panhandle, he and his dogs had killed many a wolf, and now he never doubted that, within a few days, old Lobo's scalp would dangle at his saddle-bow.

Away they went bravely on their hunt in the gray dawn of a summer morning, and soon the great dogs gave joyous tongue to say that they were already on the track of their quarry. Within two miles, the grizzly band of Currumpaw leaped into view, and the chase grew fast and furious. The part of the wolf-hounds was merely to hold the wolves at bay till the hunter could ride up and shoot them, and this usually was easy on the open plains of Texas; but here a new feature of the country came into play, and showed how well Lobo had chosen his range; for the rocky canyons of the Currumpaw and its tributaries intersect the prairies in every direction. The old wolf at once made for the nearest of these and by crossing it got rid of the horsemen. His band then scattered and thereby scattered the dogs, and when they

Tannery, with his dogs, came galloping up the cañon.

reunited at a distant point, of course, all of the dogs did not turn up, and the wolves no longer outnumbered, turned on their pursuers. and killed or desperately wounded them all. That night when Tannerey mustered his dogs, only six of them returned, and of these, two were terribly lacerated. This hunter made two other attempts to capture the royal scalp, but neither of them was more successful than the first, and on the last occasion his best horse met its death by a fall; so he gave up the chase in disgust and went back to Texas, leaving Lobo more than ever the despot of the region.

Next year, two other hunters appeared, determined to win the promised bounty. Each believed he could destroy this noted wolf, the first by means of a newly devised poison, which was to be laid out in an entirely new manner; the other a French Canadian, by poison assisted with certain spells and charms, for he firmly believed that Lobo was a veritable 'loup-garou,' and could not be killed by ordinary means. But cunningly compounded poisons, charms, and incantations were all of no avail against this grizzly devastator. He made his weekly rounds and daily banquets as aforetime, and before many weeks had passed, Calone and Laloche gave up in despair and went elsewhere to hunt.

In the spring of 1893, after his unsuccessful attempt to capture Lobo, Joe Calone had a humiliating experience, which seems to show that the big wolf simply scorned his enemies, and had absolute confidence in himself. Calone's farm was on a small tributary of the Currumpaw, in a picturesque canyon, and among the rocks of this very canyon, within a thousand yards of the house, old Lobo and his mate selected their den and raised their family that season. There they lived all summer, and killed Joe's cattle, sheep, and dogs, but laughed at all his poisons and traps, and rested securely among the recesses of the cavernous cliffs, while Joe vainly racked his brain for some method of smoking them out, or of reaching them with dynamite. But they escaped entirely unscathed, and continued their ravages as before. "There's where he lived all last summer," said Joe, pointing to the face of the cliff, "and I couldn't do a thing with him. I was like a fool to him."

II

This history, gathered so far from the cowboys, I found hard to believe until in the fall of 1893, I made the acquaintance of the wily marauder, and at length came to know him more thoroughly than anyone else. Some years before, in the Bingo days, I had been a wolf-hunter, but my occupations since then had been of another sort, chaining me to stool and desk. I was much in need of a change, and when a friend, who was also a ranch-owner on the Currumpaw, asked me to come to New Mexico and try if I could do anything with this predatory pack, I accepted the invitation and, eager to make the acquaintance of its king, was as soon as possible among the mesas of that region. I spent some time riding about to learn the country, and at intervals, my guide would point to the skeleton of a cow to which the hide still adhered, and remark, "That's some of his work."

It became quite clear to me that, in this rough country, it was useless to think of pursuing Lobo with hounds and horses, so that poison or traps were the only available expedients. At present we had no traps large enough, so I set to work with poison.

I need not enter into the details of a hundred devices that I employed to circumvent this 'loup-garou'; there was not combination of strychnine, arsenic, cyanide, or prussic acid, that I did not essay; there was no manner of flesh that I did not try as bait: but morning after morning, as I rode forth to learn the result, I found that all my efforts had been useless. The old king was too cunning for me. A single instance will show his wonderful sagacity. Acting on the hint of an old trapper, I melted some cheese together with the kidney fat of a freshly killed heifer, stewing it in a china dish, and cutting it with a bone knife to avoid the taint of metal. When the mixture was cool, I cut it into lumps, and making a hole in one side of each lump, I inserted a large dose of strychnine and cyanide, contained in a capsule that was impermeable by any odor; finally I sealed the holes up with pieces of the cheese itself. During the whole process, I wore a pair of gloves steeped in the hot blood of the heifer, and even avoided breathing on the baits. When all was ready, I put them in a rawhide bag rubbed all over with blood, and rode forth dragging the liver and kidneys of the beef at the end of a rope. With this I made a ten mile circuit, dropping a bait at each quarter of a mile, and taking the utmost care, always, not to touch any with my hands.

Lobo, generally, came into this part of the range in the early part of each week, and passed the latter part, it was supposed, around the base of Sierra Grande. This was Monday, and the same evening, as we were about to retire, I heard the deep bass howl of his majesty. On hearing it one of the boys briefly remarked, "There he is, we'll see."

The next morning I went forth, eager to know the result. I soon came on the fresh trail of the robbers, with Lobo in the lead—his track was always easily distinguished. An ordinary wolf's forefoot is 4 ½ inches long, that of a large wolf 4 ¾ inches, but Lobo's, as measured a number of times, was 5 ½ inches from claw to heel; I afterward found that his other proportions were commensurate, for he stood three feet high at the shoulder, and weighed 150 pounds. His trail, therefore, though obscured by those of his followers, was never difficult to trace. The pack had soon found the track of my drag, and as usual followed it. I could see that Lobo had come to the first bait, sniffed about it, and finally had picked it up.

Then I could not conceal my delight. "I've got him at last," I exclaimed; "I shall find him stark within a mile," and I galloped on with eager eyes fixed on the great broad track in the dust. It led me to the second bait, and that also was gone. How I exulted—I surely have him now and perhaps several of his band. But there was the broad paw-mark still on the drag; and though I stood in the stirrup and scanned the plain I saw nothing that looked like a dead wolf. Again I followed—to find now that the third bait was gone—and the king-wolf's track led on to the fourth, there to learn that he had not really taken a bait at all, but had merely carried them in his mouth. Then having piled the three on the fourth, he scattered filth over them to express his utter contempt for my devices. After this he left my drag and went about his business with the pack he guarded so effectively.

This is only one of many similar experiences which convinced me that poison would never avail to destroy this robber, and though I continued to use it while awaiting the arrival of the traps, it was only because it was meanwhile a sure means of killing many prairie wolves and other destructive vermin.

About this time there came under my observation an incident that will illustrate Lobo's diabolic cunning. These wolves had at least one pursuit which was merely an amusement, it was stampeding and killing sheep, though they rarely ate them. The sheep are usually kept in flocks of from one thousand to three thousand under one or more shepherds. At night they are gathered in the most sheltered place available, and a herdsman sleeps on each side of the flock to give additional protection. Sheep are such senseless creatures that they are liable to be stampeded by the smallest trifle, but they have deeply ingrained in their nature one, and perhaps only one, strong weakness, namely to follow their leader. And this the shepherds turn to good account by putting half a dozen goats in the flock of sheep. The latter recognize the superior intelligence of their bearded cousins, and when a night alarm occurs they crowd around them, and usually are thus saved from a stampede and are easily protected. But it was not always so. One night late in last November, two Perico shepherds were aroused by an onset of wolves. Their flocks huddled around the goats, which being neither fools or cowards, stood their ground and were bravely defiant; but alas for them, no common wolf was heading this attack. Old Lobo, the weir-wolf, knew as well as the shepherds that the goats were the moral force of the flock, so hastily running over the backs of the densely packed sheep, he fell on these leaders, slew them all in a few minutes, and soon had the luckless sheep stampeding in a thousand different directions. For weeks afterward I was almost daily accosted by some anxious shepherd, who asked, "Have you seen any stray OTO sheep lately?" and usually I was obliged to say I had; one day it was, "Yes, I came on some five or six carcasses by Diamond Springs;" or another, it was to the effect that I had seen a small 'bunch' running on the Malpai Mesa; or again, "No, but Juan Meira saw about twenty, freshly killed, on the Cedra Monte two days ago."

At length the wolf traps arrived, and with two men I worked a whole week to get them properly set out. We spared no labor or pains, I adopted every device I could think of that might help to ensure success. The

Lobo exposing the traps.

second day after the traps arrived, I rode around to inspect, and soon came upon Lobo's trail running from trap to trap. In the dust I could read the whole story of his doings that night. He had trotted along in the darkness, and although the traps were so carefully concealed, he had instantly detected the first one. Stopping the onward march of the pack, he had cautiously scratched around it until he had disclosed the trap, the chain, and the log, then left them wholly exposed to view with the trap still unsprung, and passing on he treated over a dozen traps in same fashion. Very soon I noticed that he stopped and turned aside as soon as he detected suspicious signs on the trail and a new plan to outwit him at once suggested itself. I set the traps in the form of an H; that is, with a row of traps on each side of the trail, and one on the trail for the cross-bar of the H. Before long, I had an opportunity to count another failure. Lobo came trotting along the trail, and was fairly between the parallel lines before he detected the single trap in the trail, but he stopped in time, and why or how he knew enough I cannot tell, the Angel of the wild things must have been with him, but without turning an inch to the right or left, he slowly and cautiously backed on his own tracks, putting each paw exactly in its old track until he was off the dangerous ground. Then returning at one side he scratched clods and stones with his hind feet till he had sprung every trap. This he did on many other occasions, and although I varied my methods and redoubled my precautions, he was never deceived, his sagacity seemed never at fault, and he might have been pursuing his career of rapine today, but for an unfortunate alliance that proved his ruin and added his name to the long list of heroes who, unassailable when alone, have fallen through the indiscretion of a trusted ally.

III

Once or twice, I had found indications that everything was not quite right in the Currumpaw pack. There were signs of irregularity, I thought; for instance there was clearly the trail of a smaller wolf running ahead of the leader, at times, and this I could not understand until a cowboy made a remark which explained the matter.

Lobo and Blanca.

"I saw them today," he said, "and the wild one that breaks away is Blanca." Then the truth dawned upon me, and I added. "Now, I know that Blanca is a she wolf, because were a he wolf to act thus, Lobo would kill him at once."

This suggested a new plan. I killed a heifer, and set one or two rather obvious traps about the carcass. Then cutting off the head, which is considered useless offal, and quite beneath the notice of a wolf, I set it a little apart and around it placed six powerful steel traps properly deodorized and concealed with the utmost care. During my operations I kept my hands, boots, and implements smeared with fresh blood, and afterward sprinkled the ground with the same, as though it had flowed from the head; and when the traps were buried in the dust, I brushed the place over with the skin of a coyote, and with a foot of the same animal made a number of tracks over the traps. The head was so placed that there was a narrow passage between it and some

tussocks, and in this passage I buried two of my best traps, fastening them to the head itself.

Wolves have a habit of approaching every carcass they get the wind of, in order to examine it, even when they have no intention of eating of it, and I hoped that this habit would bring the Currumpaw pack within reach of my latest stratagem. I did not doubt that Lobo would detect my handiwork about the meat, and prevent the pack approaching it, but I did build some hopes on the head, for it looked as though it had been thrown aside as useless. Next morning, I sallied forth to inspect the traps, and there, oh, joy! were the tracks of the pack, and the place where the beef-head and its traps had been was empty. A hasty study of the trail showed that Lobo had kept the pack from approaching the meat, but one, a small wolf, had evidently gone on to examine the head as it lay apart and had walked right into one of the traps.

We set out on the trail, and within a mile discovered that the hapless wolf was Blanca. Away she went, however, at a gallop, and although encumbered by the beef head, which weighed over fifty pounds, she speedily distanced my companion who was on foot. But we overtook her when she reached the rocks, for the horns of the cow's head became caught and held her fast. She was the handsomest wolf I had ever seen. Her coat was in perfect condition and nearly white.

She turned to fight, and raising her voice in the rallying cry of her race, sent a long howl rolling over the canyon. From far away upon the mesa came a deep response, the cry of Old Lobo. That was her last call, for now we had closed in on her, and all her energy and breath were devoted to combat.

Then followed the inevitable tragedy, the idea of which I shrank from afterward more than at the time. We each threw a lasso over the neck of the doomed wolf, and strained out horses in opposite directions until the blood burst from her mouth, her eyes glazed, her limbs stiffened and then fell limp. Homeward then we rode, carrying the dead wolf, and exulting over this, the first death-blow we had been able to inflict on the Currumpaw pack.

At intervals during the tragedy, and afterward as we rode homeward, we heard the roar of Lobo as he wandered about on the distant mesas, where he seemed to be searching for Blanca. He had never really deserted her, but knowing that he could not save her, his deep-rooted dread of firearms had been too much for him when he saw us approaching. All that day we heard him wailing as he roamed in his quest, and I remarked at length to one of the boys, "Now, indeed, I truly know that Blanca was his mate."

As evening fell he seemed to be coming toward the home canyon, for his voice sounded continually nearer. There was an unmistakable note of sorrow in it now. It was no longer the loud, defiant howl, but a long, plaintive wail; "Blanca! Blanca!" he seemed to call. And as night came down, I noticed that he was not far from the place where we had overtaken her. At length he seemed to find the trail, and when he came to the spot where we had killed her, his heart-broken wailing was piteous to hear. It was sadder than I could possibly have believed. Even the stolid cowboys noticed it, and said they had "never heard a wolf carry on like that before." He seemed to know exactly what had taken place, for her blood had stained the place of her death.

Then he took up the trail of the horses and followed it to the ranch-house. Whether in hopes of finding her there, or in quest of revenge, I know not, but the latter was what he found, for he surprised our unfortunate watchdog outside and tore him to little bits within fifty yards of the door. He evidently came alone this time, for I found but one trail next morning, and he had galloped about in a reckless manner that was very unusual with him. I had half expected this, and had set a number of additional traps about the pasture. Afterward I found that he had indeed fallen into one of these, but such was his strength, he had torn himself loose and cast it aside.

I believed that he would continue in the neighborhood until he found her body at least, so I concentrated all my energies on this one enterprise of catching him before he left the region, and while yet in this reckless mood. Then I realized what a mistake I had made in killing Blanca, for by using her as a decoy, I might have secured him the next night.

I gathered in all the traps I could command, one hundred and thirty strong steel wolf-traps, and set them in fours in every trail that led into the canyon; each trap was separately fastened to a log, and each log was separately buried. In burying them, I carefully removed the sod and every particle of earth that was lifted we put in blankets, so that after the sod was replaced and all was finished the eye could detect no trace of human handiwork. When the traps were concealed I trailed the body of poor Blanca over each place, and made of it a drag that circled all about the ranch, and finally I took off one of her paws and made with it a line of tracks over each trap. Every precaution and device known to me I used, and retired at a late hour to await the result.

Once during the night I thought I heard Old Lobo, but was not sure of it. Next day I rode around, but darkness came on before I completed the circuit of the north canyon, and I had nothing to report. At supper one of the cowboys said, "There was a great row among the cattle in the north canyon this morning, maybe there is something in the traps there." It was afternoon of the next day before I got to the place referred to, and as I drew near a great grizzly form arose from the ground, vainly endeavoring to escape, and there revealed before me stood Lobo, King of the Currumpaw, firmly held in the traps. Poor old hero, he had never ceased to search for his darling, and when he found the trail her body had made he followed it recklessly, and so fell into the snare prepared for him. There he lay in the iron grasp of all four traps, perfectly helpless, and all around him were numerous tracks showing how the cattle had gathered about him to insult the fallen despot, without daring to approach within his reach. For two days and two nights he had lain there, and now was worn out with struggling. Yet, when I went near him, he rose up with bristling mane and raised his voice, and for the last time made the canyon reverberate with his deep bass roar, a call for help, the muster call of his band. But there was none to answer him, and, left alone in his extremity, he whirled about with all his strength and made a desperate effort to get at me. All in vain, each trap was a dead drag of over three hundred pounds, and in their relentless four-fold grasp, with great steel jaws on every foot, and the heavy logs and chains all entangled together, he was absolutely powerless, how his huge ivory tusks did grind on those cruel chains, and when I ventured to touch him with my rifle barrel he left grooves on it which are there to this day. His eyes glared green with hate and fury, and his jaws snapped with a hollow "chop," as he vainly endeavored to reach me and my trembling horse. But he was worn out with hunger and struggling and loss of blood, and he soon sank exhausted to the ground.

Something like compunction came over me, as I prepared to deal out to him that which so many had suffered at his hands.

"Grand old outlaw, hero of a thousand lawless raids, in a few minutes you will be but a great load of carrion. It cannot be otherwise." Then I swung my lasso and sent it whistling over his head. But not so fast; he was yet far from being subdued, and, before the supple coils had fallen on his neck he seized the noose and, with one fierce chop, cut through its hard thick strands, and dropped it in two pieces at his feet.

Of course I had my rifle as a last resource, but I did not wish to spoil his royal hide, so I galloped back to the camp and returned with a cowboy and a fresh lasso. We threw to our victim a stick of wood which he seized in his teeth, and before he could relinquish it our lassoes whistled through the air and tightened on his neck.

Yet before the light had died from his fierce eyes, I cried, "Stay, we will not kill him; let us take him alive to the camp." He was so completely powerless now that it was easy to put a stout stick through his mouth, behind his tusks, and then lash his jaws with a heavy cord which was also fastened to the stick. The stick kept the cord in, and the cord kept the stick in so he was harmless. As soon as he felt his jaws were tied he made no further resistance, and uttered no sound, but looked calmly at us and seemed to say, "Well, you have got me at last, do as you please with me." And from that time he took no more notice of us.

We tied his feet securely, but he never groaned, nor growled, nor turned his head. Then with our united strength were just able to put him on my horse. His breath came evenly as though sleeping, and his eyes were bright and clear again, but did not rest on us. Afar on the great rolling mesas they were fixed, his passing kingdom, where his famous band was now scattered. And he gazed till the pony descended the pathway into the canyon, and the rocks cut off the view.

By traveling slowly we reached the ranch in safety, and after securing him with a collar and a strong chain, we staked him out in the pasture and removed the cords. Then for the first time I could examine him closely, and proved how unreliable is vulgar report when a living hero or tyrant is concerned. He had not a collar of gold about his neck, nor was there on his shoulders an inverted cross to denote that he had leagued himself with Satan. But I did find on one haunch a great broad scar, that tradition says was the fang mark of Juno, the leader of Tannerey's wolf hounds—a mark which she gave him the moment before he stretched her lifeless on the sand of the canyon.

I set meat and water beside him, but he paid no heed. He lay calmly on his breast, and gazed with those steadfast yellow eyes away past me down through the gateway of the canyon, over the open plains—his plains—nor moved a muscle when I touched him. When the sun went down he was still gazing fixedly across the prairie. I expected he would call up his band when night came, and prepared for them, but he had called once in his extremity, and none had come; he would never call again.

A lion shorn of his strength, an eagle robbed of his freedom, or a dove bereft of his mate, all die, it is said, of a broken heart; and who will aver that this grim bandit could bear the three-fold brunt, heart-whole? This only I know, that when the morning dawned, he was lying there still in his position of calm repose, his body unwounded, but his spirit was gone—the old King-wolf was dead.

I took the chain from his neck, a cowboy helped me to carry him to the shed where lay the remains of Blanca, and as we laid him beside her, the cattleman exclaimed, "There, you would come to her, now you are together again."

The Pacing Mustang

While hunting wolves in New Mexico in the fall of 1893, Seton heard a story about a pacing mustang that lived a short distance south of Lobo's range. He later recounted the story as part of *Wild Animals I Have Known* and wrote in the introduction of the book that he related the story virtually as he heard it.

Seton's story is notable in that it includes an accurate description of the various techniques employed by mustangers in the West to capture wild horses.

In the history of the American West there are several stories about pacing mustang stallions, all of them similar to Seton's. Nevertheless, they differ from Seton's in two important aspects. First, all of the horses in the frontier accounts were white, while Seton's stallion was shiny coal black. More importantly, the stallions in the frontier accounts were successful in evading capture because their pacing gait enabled them to outdistance their would-be captors. Such was not the case with the black stallion of Seton's story.

In his autobiography, *Trail of An Artist-Naturalist*, Seton related that some years after he heard the Pacing Mustang story, he met a man who was present at the stallion's capture. The former cowboy informed Seton that he had read his story in *Wild Animals I Have Known* and that it followed closely actual events except for the ending.

According to the cowboy, after the stallion was captured, he was taken to a nearby ranch that was equipped with corrals. There, he was roped by the cowboys, thrown, and saddled. Tom Turkeytrack, although sixty-five years old, then decided to carry out his own bronc busting.

After several turns around the corral riding the raging stallion, Old Tom asked that the gate to the corral be opened, and the horse allowed to run in open country. When the stallion came to a deep canyon, however, he jumped off the edge, taking his tormentor to death with him. Seton remarked that he felt that this version was a better way to end the tale and lamented that he had not known about it when he wrote the story.

Range historian J. Frank Dobie, who collected a number of the historic pacing stallion stories in his book, *The Mustangs,* described Seton's story as being "beautiful and true to range men as well as horses."

The Pacing Mustang

I

o Calone threw down his saddle on the dusty ground, turned his horses loose, and went clanking into the ranch house.

"Nigh about chuck time?" he asked.

"Seventeen minutes," said the cook glancing at the Waterbury, with the air of a train-starter, though this show of precision had never yet been justified by events.

"How's things on the Perico?" said Jo's pard.

"Hotter'n hinges," said Jo. "Cattle seem O.K.; lots of calves."

"I seen that bunch o'mustangs that waters at Antelope Springs; couple o' colts along; one little dark one, a fair dandy; a born pacer. I run them a mile or two, and he led the bunch, an' never broke his pace. Cut loose, an' pushed them jest for fun, an' darned if I could make him break."

"You didn't have no reefreshments along?" Said Scarth, incredulously.

"That's all right, Scarth. You had to crawl on our last bet, an' you'll get another chance soon as you're man enough."

"Chuck," shouted the cook, and the subject was dropped. Next day the scene of the roundup was changed, and the mustangs were forgotten.

A year later the same corner of New Mexico was worked over by the roundup, and again the mustang bunch was seen. The dark colt was now a black yearling, with thin, clean legs and glossy flanks; and more than one of the boys saw with his own eyes this oddity—the mustang was a born pacer.

Jo was along, and the idea now struck him that that colt was worth having. To an Easterner this thought may not seem startling or original, but in the West, where an unbroken horse is worth $5, and where an ordinary saddle horse is worth $15 or $20, the idea of a wild mustang being desirable property does not occur to the average cowboy, for mustangs are hard to catch, and when caught are merely wild animal prisoners, perfectly useless and untamable to the last. Not a few of the cattle owners make a point of shooting all mustangs at sight, for they are not only useless cumberers of the feeding grounds, but commonly lead away domestic horses, which soon take to the wild life and are thenceforth lost.

Wild Jo Calone knew a 'bronk right down to subsoil.' "I never seen a white that wasn't soft, nor a chestnut that wasn't nervous, nor a bay that wasn't good if broke right, nor a black that wasn't hard as nails, an' full of the old Harry. All a black bronk wants is claws to be wus'n Daniel's hull outfit of lions."

Since then a mustang is worthless vermin, and black mustang ten times worse that worthless, Jo's pard "didn't see no sense in Jo's wantin' to corral the yearling," as he now seemed intent on doing. But Jo got no chance to try that year.

He was only a cowpuncher on $25 a month, and tied to hours. Like most of the boys, he always looked forward to having a ranch and an outfit of his own. His brand, the hogpen, of sinister suggestion, was already registered at Santa Fe, but of horned stock it was borne by a single old cow, so as to give him a legal right to put his brand on any maverick (or unbranded animal) he might chance to find.

Yet each fall, when paid off, Jo could not resist the temptation to go to town with the boys and have a good time 'while the stuff held out.' So that his property consisted of little more than his saddle, his bed, and his old cow. He kept on hoping to make a strike that would leave him well fixed with a fair start, and when the thought came that the Black Mustang was his mascot, he only needed a chance to 'make the try.'

The roundup circled down to the Canadian River, and back in the fall by the Don Carlos Hills, and Jo saw no more of the Pacer, though he heard of him from many quarters; for the colt, now a vigorous young horse, rising three, was beginning to be talked of.

Antelope Springs is in the middle of a great plain. When the water is high it spreads into a small lake with a belt of sedge around it; when it is low there is a wide flat of black mud, glistening white with alkali in places, and the spring a water hole in the middle. It has no flow or outlet and yet is fairly good water, the only drinking place for many miles.

This flat, or prairie as it would be called farther north, was the favorite feeding ground of the Black Stallion, but it was also the pasture of many herds of range horses and cattle. Chiefly interested was the L Cross F outfit. Foster, the manager and part owner, was a man of enterprise. He believed it would pay to handle a better class of cattle and horses on the range, and one of his ventures was ten half-blooded mares, tall, clean limbed, deer-eyed creatures, that made the scrub cow ponies look like pitiful starvelings of some degenerate and quite different species.

One of these was kept stabled for use, but the nine, after the weaning of their colts, managed to get away and wandered off on the range.

A horse has a fine instinct for the road to the best feed, and the nine mares drifted, of course, to the prairie of Antelope Springs, twenty miles to the southward. And when, later that summer Foster went to round them up, he found the nine indeed, but with them and guarding them with an air of more than mere comradeship was a coal-black stallion, prancing around and rounding up the bunch like an expert, his jet-black coat a vivid contrast to the golden hides of his harem.

The mares were gentle, and would have been easily driven homeward but for a new and unexpected thing. The Black Stallion became greatly aroused. He seemed to inspire them too with his wildness, and flying this way and that way, drove the whole band at full gallop where he would. Away they went, and the little cow ponies that carried the men were easily left behind.

This was maddening, and both men at last drew their guns and sought a chance to drop that 'blasted stallion.' But no chance came that was not nine to one of dropping one of the mares. A long day of maneuvering made no change. The Pacer, for it was he, kept his family together and disappeared among the southern sand hills. The cattlemen on their jaded ponies set out for home with the poor satisfaction of vowing vengeance for their failure on the superb cause of it.

One of the most aggravating parts of it was that one or two experiences like this would surely make the mares as wild as the mustang, and there seemed to be no way of saving them from it.

Scientists differ on the power of beauty and prowess to attract female admiration among the lower animals, but whether it is admiration or the prowess itself, it is certain that a wild animal of uncommon gifts soon wins a large following from the harems of his rivals. And the great Black Horse, with his inky mane and tail and his green-lighted eyes, ranged through all that region and added to his following from many bands till not less than a score of mares were in his bunch. Most were merely humble cow ponies turned out to range, but the nine great mares were there, a striking group by themselves. According to all reports, this bunch was always kept rounded up and guarded with such energy and jealously that a mare, once in it, was a lost animal so far as man was concerned, and the ranchmen realized soon that they had gotten on the range a mustang that was doing them more harm than all other sources of loss put together.

II

It was December, 1893. I was new in the country, and was setting out from the ranch house on the Pinavetitos, to go with a wagon to the Canadian River. As I was leaving, Foster finished his remark by, "And if you get a chance to draw a bead on that accursed mustang, don't fail to drop him in his tracks."

This was the first I had heard of him, and as I rode along I gathered from Burns, my guide, the history that has been given. I was full of curiosity to see the famous three-year-old, and was not a little disappointed on the second day when we came to the prairie on Antelope Springs and saw no sign of the Pacer or his band.

But on the next day, as we crossed the Alamosa Arroyo, and were rising to the rolling prairie again, Jack Burns, who was riding on ahead, suddenly dropped flat on the neck of his horse, and swung back to me in the wagon, saying;

"Get out your rifle, here's that —— stallion."

I seized my rifle, and hurried forward to view over the prairie ridge. In the hollow below was a band of horses, and there at one end was the Great Black Mustang. He had heard some sound of our approach, and was not unsuspicious of danger. There, he stood with head and tail erect, and nostrils wide, an image of horse perfection and beauty, as noble an animal as ever ranged the plains, and the mere notion of turning that magnificent creature into a mass of carrion was horrible. In spite of Jack's exhortation to 'shoot quick,' I delayed, and threw open the breach, whereupon he, always hot and hasty, swore at my slowness, growled, 'Gi' me that gun,' and as he seized it I turned the muzzle up, and accidently the gun went off.

Instantly the herd below was all alarm, the great black leader snorted and neighed and dashed about. And the mares bunched, and away all went in a rumble of hoofs and a cloud of dust.

The Stallion careered now on this side, now on that, and kept his eye on all and led and drove them far away. As long as I could see, I watched and never once did he break his pace.

Jack made Western remarks about me and my gun, as well as that mustang, but I rejoiced in the Pacer's strength and beauty, and not for all the mares in the bunch would I have harmed his glossy hide.

III

There are several ways of capturing wild horses. One is by creasing—that is, grazing the animal's nape with a rifle ball so that he is stunned long enough for hobbling.

"Yes! I seen about a hundred necks broke trying it, but I never seen a mustang creased yet," was Wild Jo's critical remark.

Sometimes, if the shape of the country abets it, the herd can be driven into a corral; sometimes with extra fine mounts they can be run down, but by far the commonest way, paradoxical as it may seem, is to walk them down.

The fame of the Stallion that never was known to gallop was spreading. Extraordinary stories were told of his gait, his speed, and his wind, and when old Montgomery of the Triangle Bar outfit came out plum at Well's Hotel in Clayton, and in presence of witnesses said he'd give one thousand dollars cash for him safe in a box car, providing the stories were true, a dozen young cowpunchers were eager to cut loose and win the purse, as soon as present engagements were up. But Wild Jo had had his eye on this very deal for quite a while; there was no time to lose, so ignoring present contracts he rustled all night to raise the necessary equipment for the game.

By straining his already overstrained credit, and taxing the already overtaxed generosity of his friends, he got together an expedition consisting of twenty good saddle horses, a mess wagon, and fortnight's stuff for three men—himself, his pard, Charley, and the cook.

Then they set out from Clayton, with the avowed intention of walking down the wonderfully swift wild horse. The third day they arrived at Antelope Springs, and as it was about noon they were not surprised to see the Black Pacer marching down to drink with all his band behind him. Jo kept out of sight until the wild horses each and all had drunk their fill, for a thirsty animal always travels better than one laden with water.

Jo then rode quietly forward. The Pacer took alarm at half a mile, and led his band away out of sight on the soapweed mesa to the southeast. Jo followed at a gallop till he once more sighted them, then came back and instructed the cook, who was also teamster, to make for Alamosa Arroyo in the south. Then away to the southeast he went after the mustangs. After a mile or two he once more sighted them, and walked his horse quietly till so near that they again took alarm and circled away to the south. An hour's trot, not on the trail, but cutting across to where they ought to go, brought Jo again in close sight. Again he walked quietly toward the herd, and again there was the alarm and flight. And so they passed the afternoon, but circled ever more and more to the south, so that when the sun was low they were, as Jo had expected, not far from Alamosa Arroyo. The band was again close at hand, and Jo, after starting them off, rode to the wagon, while his pard, who had been taking it easy, took up the slow chase on a fresh horse.

After supper the wagon moved on to the upper ford of the Alamosa, as arranged, and there camped for the night.

Meanwhile, Charley followed the herd. They had not run so far as at first, for their pursuer made no sign of attack, and they were getting used to his company. They were more easily found, as the shadows fell, on account of a snow-white mare that was in the bunch. A young moon in the sky now gave some help, and relying on his horse to choose the path, Charley kept him quietly walking after the herd, represented by that ghost-white mare, till they were lost in the night. He then got off, unsaddled and picketed his horse, and in his blanket quickly went to sleep.

At the first streak of dawn he was up, and within a short half mile, thanks to the snowy mare, he found the band. At his approach, the shrill neigh of the Pacer bugled his troop into a flying squad. But on the first mesa they stopped, and faced about to see what this persistent follower was, and what he wanted. For a moment or so they stood against the sky to gaze, and then deciding that he knew him as well as he wished to, that black meteor flung his mane on the wind, and led off at his tireless, even swing, while the mares came streaming after.

Away they went, circling now to the west, and after several repetitions of this same play, flying, following, and overtaking, and flying again, they passed, near noon, the old Apache look out, Buffalo Bluff. And here, on watch, was Jo. A long thin column of smoke told Charley to come to camp, and with a flashing pocket mirror he made response.

Jo, freshly mounted, rode across, and again took up the chase, and back came Charley to camp to eat and rest, and then move on up stream.

All that day Jo followed, and managed, when it was needed, that the herd should keep the great circle, of which the wagon cut a small chord. At sundown he came to Verde Crossing, and there was Charley with a fresh horse and food, and Jo went on in the same calm, dogged way. All the evening he followed, and far into the night, for the wild herd was now getting somewhat used to the presence of the harmless strangers, and were more easily followed; moreover, they were tiring out with perpetual traveling. They were no longer in the good grass country, they were not grain fed like the horses on their track, and above all, the slight but continuous nervous tension was surely telling. It spoiled their appetites, but made them very thirsty. They were allowed, and as far as possible encouraged, to drink deeply at every chance. The effect of large quantities of water on a running animal is well known; it tends to stiffen the limbs and spoil the wind. Jo carefully guarded his own horse against such excess, and both he and his horse were fresh when they camped that night on the trail of the jaded mustangs.

At dawn he found them easily close at hand, and though they ran at first they did not go far before they dropped into a walk. The battle seemed nearly won now, for the chief difficulty in the 'walk-down' is to keep track of the herd the first two or three days when they are fresh.

All that morning Jo kept in sight, generally in close sight, of the band. About ten o'clock, Charley relieved him near Jose Peak and that day the mustangs walked only a quarter of a mile ahead with much less spirit than the day before and circled now more north again. At night Charley was supplied with a fresh horse and followed as before.

Next day the mustangs walked with heads held low, and, in spite of the efforts of the Black Pacer, at times they were less than a hundred yards ahead of their pursuer.

The fourth and fifth days passed the same way, and now the herd was nearly back to Antelope Springs. So far all had come out as expected. The chase had been in a great circle with the wagon following the lesser circle.

The wild herd was back to its starting point, worn out; and the hunters were back, fresh and on fresh horses. The herd was kept from drinking till late in the afternoon and then driven to the Springs to swell themselves with a perfect water gorge. Now was the chance for the skillful ropers on the grain fed horses to close in, for the sudden heavy drink was ruination, almost paralysis, of wind and limb, and it would be easy to rope and hobble them one by one.

There was only one weak spot in the program, the Black Stallion, the cause of the hunt, seemed made of iron, that ceaseless swinging pace seemed as swift and vigorous now as on the morning when the chase began. Up and down he went rounding up the herd and urging them on by voice and example to escape. But they were played out. The old white mare that had been such help in sighting them at night, had dropped out hours ago, dead beat. The half-bloods seemed to be losing all fear of the horsemen, the band was clearly in Jo's power. But the one who was the prize of all the hunt seemed just as far as ever out of reach.

Here was a puzzle. Jo's comrades knew him well and would not have been surprised to see him in a sudden rage attempt to shoot the Stallion down. But Jo had no such mind. During that long week of following he had watched the horse all day at speed and never once had he seen him gallop.

The horseman's adoration of a noble horse had grown and grown, till now he would as soon have thought of shooting his best mount as firing on that splendid beast.

Jo even asked himself whether he would take the handsome sum that was offered for the prize. Such an animal would be a fortune in himself to sire a race of pacers for the track.

But the prize was still at large—the time had come to finish up the hunt. Jo's finest mount was caught. She was a mare of Eastern blood, but raised on the plains. She never would have come into Jo's possession but for a curious weakness. The loco is a poisonous weed that grows in these regions. Most stock will not touch it; but sometimes an animal tries it and becomes addicted to it. It acts somewhat like morphine, but the animal, though sane for long intervals, has always a passion for the herb and finally dies mad. A beast with the craze is said to be locoed. And Jo's best mount had a wild gleam in her eye that to an expert told the tale.

But she was swift and strong and Jo chose her for the grand finish of the chase. It would have been an easy matter now to rope the mares, but was no longer necessary. They could be separated from their black leader and driven home to the corral. But that leader still had the look of untamed strength. Jo, rejoicing in a worthy foe, went bounding forth to try the odds. The lasso was flung on the ground and trailed to take out every kink, and gathered as he rode into neatest coils across his left palm. Then putting on the spur the first time in the chase he rode straight for the Stallion a quarter of a mile beyond. Away he went, and away went Jo, each at his best, while the fagged-out mares scattered right and left and let them pass. Straight across the open plain the fresh horse went at its hardest gallop, and the Stallion, leading off, still kept his start and kept his famous swing.

It was incredible, and Jo put on more spur and shouted to his horse, which fairly flew, but shortened up the space between by not a single inch. For the Black One whirled across the flat and up and passed a soapweed mesa and down across a sandy treacherous plain, then over a grassy stretch where prairie dogs barked, then hid below, and on came Jo, but there to see, could he believe his eyes, the Stallion's start grown longer still, and Jo began to curse his luck, and urge and spur his horse until the poor uncertain brute got into such a state of nervous fright, her eyes began to roll, she wildly shook her head from side to side, no longer picked her ground—a badger hole received her foot and down she went, and Jo went flying to the earth. Though badly bruised, he gained his feet and tried to mount his crazy beast. But she, poor brute, was done for—her off foreleg hung loose.

There was but one thing to do. Jo loosed the cinch, put Lightfoot out of pain, and carried back the saddle to the camp. While the Pacer streamed away till lost to view.

This was not quite defeat, for all the mares were manageable now, and Jo and Charley drove them carefully to the L Cross F corral and claimed a good reward. But Jo was more than ever bound to own the Stallion. He had seen what stuff he was made of, he prized him more and more, and only sought to strike some better plan to catch him.

IV

The cook on that trip was Bates—Mr. Thomas Bates, he called himself at the post office where he regularly went for the letters and remittance which never came. Old Tom Turkeytrack, the boys called him, from his cattle brand, which he said was on record at Denver, and which, according to his story, was also borne by countless beef and saddle stock on the plains of the unknown North.

When asked to join the trip as a partner, Bates made some sarcastic remarks about horses not fetching $12 a dozen, which had been literally true within the year, and he preferred to go on a very meager salary. But no one who once saw the Pacer going had failed to catch the craze. Turkeytrack experienced the usual change of heart. He now wanted to own that mustang. How this was to be brought about he did not clearly see till one day there called at the ranch that had 'secured his services,' as he put it, one, Bill Smith, more usually known as Horseshoe Billy, from his cattle brand. While the excellent fresh beef and bread and the vile coffee, dried peaches and molasses were being consumed, he of the horseshoe remarked, in tones which percolated through a huge stop gap of bread;

"Wall, I seen that thar Pacer today, nigh enough to put a plait in his tail."

"What, you didn't shoot?"

"No, but I come might near it."

"Don't you be led into no sich foolishness," said a Double Bar H cowpuncher at the other end of the table. "I calc'late that maverick 'ill carry my brand before the moon changes."

"You'll have to be pretty spry or you'll find a Triangle Dot on his weather side when you get there."

"Where did you run acrost him?"

"Wall, it was like this. I was riding the flat by Antelope Springs and I sees a lump on the dry mud inside the rush belt. I knowed I never seen that before, so rides up, thinking it might be some of our stock, an' seen it was a horse lying plumb flat. The wind was blowing from him to me, so I rides up close and seen it was the Pacer, dead as a mackerel. Still, he didn't look swelled or cut, and there wa'n't no smell, an' I didn't know what to think till I seen his ear twitch off a fly and then I knowed he was sleeping. I gits down me a rope and coils it, and seen it was old and pretty shaky in spots, and me saddle a single cinch, an' me pony about 700 again a 1,200 pound stallion, an' I sez to meself, sez I, 'Tain't no use, I'll only break me cinch and git throwed an' lose me saddle.' So I hits the saddle horn a crack with the honda, and I wish't you'd a seen that mustang. He lept six foot in the air an' snorted like he was shunting cars. His eyes fairly bugged out an' he lighted out lickety split for California, and he orter be there about now if he kep' on like he started— and I swear he never made a break the hull trip."

The story was not quite so consecutive as given here. It was much punctuated by present engrossments, and from first to last was more or less infiltrated through the necessaries of life, for Bill was a healthy young man without a trace of false shame. But the account was complete and everyone believed it, for Billy was known to be reliable. Of all those who heard, old Turkeytrack talked the least and probably thought the most, for it gave him a new idea.

During his after dinner pipe he studied it out and deciding that he could not go it alone, he took Horseshoe Billy into his council and the result was a partnership in a new venture to capture the Pacer; that is, the $5,000 that was now said to be the offer for him safe in a box car.

Antelope Springs was still the usual watering place of the Pacer. The water being low left a broad belt of dry black mud between the sedge and the spring. At two places this belt was broken by a well marked trail made by the animals coming to drink. Horses and wild animals usually kept to these trails, though the horned cattle had no hesitation in taking a short cut through the sedge.

In the most used of these trails the two men set to work with shovels and dug a pit fifteen feet long, six feet wide and seven feet deep. It was a hard twenty hours work for them as it had to be completed between the Mustang's drinks, and it began to be very damp work before it was finished. With poles, brush, and earth it was then cleverly covered over and concealed. And the men went to a distance and hid in pits made for the purpose.

About noon the Pacer came, alone now since the capture of his band. The trail on the opposite side of the mud belt was little used, and old Tom, by throwing some fresh rushes across it, expected to make sure that the Stallion would enter by the other, if indeed he should by any caprice try to come by the unusual path.

What sleepless Angel is it watches over and cares for the wild animals? In spite of all reasons to take the usual path, the Pacer came along the other. The suspicious looking rushes did not stop him; he walked calmly to the water and drank. There was only one way now to prevent utter failure. When he lowered his head for the second draft which horses always take, Bates and Smith quit their holes and ran swiftly toward the trail behind him, and when he raised his proud head Smith sent a revolver shot into the ground behind him.

Away went the Pacer at his famous gait straight to the trap. Another second and he would be into it. Already he is on the trail, and already they feel they have him, but the Angel of the wild things is with him, that incomprehensible warning comes, and with one mighty bound he clears the fifteen feet of treacherous ground and spurns the earth as he fades away unharmed, never again to visit Antelope Springs by either of the beaten paths.

V

Wild Jo never lacked energy. He meant to catch that Mustang, and when he learned that others were bestirring themselves for the same purpose he at once set about trying the best untried plan he knew—the plan by which the coyote catches the fleeter jackrabbit, and mounted Indian the far swifter antelope—the old plan of the relay chase.

The Canadian river on the south, its affluent, the Pinavetitos Arroyo, on the northeast, and the Don Carlos Hills with the Ute Creek Canyon on the west, formed a sixty mile triangle that was the range of the Pacer. It was believed that he never went outside this, and at all times

Antelope Springs was his headquarters. Jo knew this country well, all the water holes and canyon crossings as well as the ways of the Pacer.

If he could have gotten fifty good horses he could have posted them to advantage so as to cover all points, but twenty mounts and five good riders were all that proved available.

The horses, grain fed for two weeks before, were sent on ahead; each man was instructed now to play his part and sent to his post the day before the race. On the day of the start Jo with his wagon drove to the plain of Antelope Springs and, camping far off in a little draw, waited.

At last he came, that coal black horse, out from the sand hills at the south, alone as always now, and walked calmly down to the Springs and circled quite around it to sniff for any hidden foe. Then he approached where there was no trail at all and drank.

Jo watched and wished he would drink a hogshead. But the moment that he turned and sought the grass Jo spurred his steed. The Pacer heard the hoofs, then saw the running horse, and did not want a nearer view but led away. Across the flat he went down to the south, and kept the famous swinging gait that made his start grow longer. Now through the sandy dunes he went, and steadying to an even pace he gained considerably and Jo's too laden horse plunged through the sand and sinking fetlock deep, he lost at every bound. Then came a level stretch where the runner seemed to gain, and then a long decline where Jo's horse dared not run his best, so lost again at every step.

But on they went, and Jo spared neither spur nor quirt. A mile—a mile—and another mile, and the far off rock at Arriba loomed up ahead.

And there Jo knew fresh mounts were held, and on they dashed. But the night black mane out level on the breeze ahead was gaining more and more.

Arriba Canyon reached at last, the watcher stood aside, for it was not wished to turn the race, and the Stallion passed—dashed down, across and up the slope, with that unbroken pace, the only one he knew.

And Jo came bounding on his foaming steed, and leaped on the waiting mount, then urged him down the slope and up upon the track, and on the upland once more drove in the spurs, and raced and raced, and raced, but not a single inch he gained.

Ga-lump, ga-lump, ga-lump with measured beat he went—an hour, and another hour—Arroyo Alamosa just ahead with fresh relays, and Jo yelled at his horse and pushed him on and on. Straight for the place the Black One made, but on the last two miles some strange foreboding turned him to the left, and Jo foresaw escape in this, and pushed his jaded mount at any cost to head him off, and hard as they had raced this was the hardest race of all, with gasps for breath and leather squeaks at every straining bound. Then cutting right across, Jo seemed to gain, and drawing his gun he fired shot after shot to toss the dust, and so turned the Stallion's head and forced him back to take the crossing to the right.

Down they went. The Stallion crossed and Jo sprang to the ground. His horse was done, for thirty miles had passed in the last stretch, and Jo himself was worn out. His eyes were burnt with flying alkali dust. He half blind so he motioned to his pard to "go ahead and keep him straight for Alamosa ford."

Out shot the rider on a strong, fresh steed, and away they went—up and down on the rolling plain— the Black Horse flecked with snowy foam. His heaving

Away went the mustang at his famous pace.

ribs and noisy breath showed what he felt—but on and on he went.

And Tom on Ginger seemed to gain, then lose and lose, when in an hour the long decline of Alamosa came. And there a freshly mounted lad took up the chase and turned it west, and on they went past towns of prairie dogs, through soapweed tracts and cactus brakes by scores, and pricked and wrenched rode on. With dust and sweat the Black was now a dappled brown, but still he stepped the same. Young Carrington, who followed, had hurt his steed by pushing at the very start, and spurred and urged him now to cut across a gulch at which the Pacer shied. Just one misstep and down they went.

The boy escaped, but the pony lies there yet, and the wild Black Horse kept on.

This was close to old Gallego's ranch where Jo himself had cut across refreshed to push the chase. Within thirty minutes he was again scorching the Pacer's trail.

Far in the west the Carlos Hills were seen, and there Jo knew fresh men and mounts were waiting, and that way the indomitable rider tried to turn the race, but by a sudden whim, of the inner warning born perhaps, the Pacer turned. Sharp to the north he went, and Jo, the skillful wrangler, rode and rode and yelled and tossed the dust with shots, but down a gulch the wild black meteor streamed and Jo could only follow. Then came the hardest race of all; Jo, cruel to the Mustang, was crueller to his mount and to himself. The sun was hot, the scorching plain was dim in shimmering heat, his eyes and lips were burnt with sand and salt, and yet the chase sped on. The only chance to win would be if he could drive the Mustang back to Big Arroyo Crossing. Now almost for the first time he saw signs of weakening in the Black. His mane and tail were not just quite so high, and his short half mile of start was down by more than half, but still he stayed ahead and paced and paced and paced.

An hour and another hour, and still they went the same. But they turned again, and night was near when big Arroyo ford was reached—fully twenty miles. But Jo was game, he seized the waiting horse. The one he left went gasping to the stream and gorged himself with water till he died.

Then Jo held back in hopes the foaming Black would drink. But he was wise; he gulped a single gulp, splashed through the stream and then passed on with Jo at speed behind him. And when they last were seen the Black was on ahead just out of reach and Jo's horse bounding on.

It was morning when Jo came to camp on foot. His tale was briefly told—eight horses dead—five men worn out—the matchless Pacer safe and free.

"Taint possible; it can't be done. Sorry I didn't bore his hellish carcass through when I had the chance," said Jo, and gave it up.

VI

Old Turkeytrack was cook on this trip. He had watched the chase with as much interest as anyone, and when it failed he grinned into the pot and said, "That mustang's mine unless I'm a darned fool." Then falling back on Scripture for a precedent, as was his habit, he still addressed the pot;

"Reckon the Philistines tried to run Samson down and they got done up, an' would a stayed done only for a nat'ral weakness on his part. An' Adam would a loafed in Eden yit only for a leetle failing which we all onderstand. An' it ain't $5,000 I'll take for him nuther."

Much persecution had made the Pacer wilder than ever. But it did not drive him away from Antelope Springs. That was the only drinking place with absolutely no shelter for a mile on every side to hide an enemy. Here he came almost every day about noon, and after thoroughly spying the land approached to drink.

His had been a lonely life all winter since the capture of his harem, and of this old Turkeytrack was fully aware. The old cook's chum had a nice little brown mare which he judged would serve his ends, and taking a pair of the strongest hobbles, a spade, a spare lasso, and a stout post he mounted the mare and rode away to the famous Springs.

A few antelope skimmed over the plain before him in the early freshness of the day. Cattle were lying about in groups, and the loud, sweet song of the prairie lark was heard on every side. For the bright snow-less winter of the mesas was gone and the springtime was at hand. The grass was greening and all nature seemed turning to thoughts of love.

It was in the air, and when the little brown mare was picketed out to graze she raised her nose from time to time to pour forth a long shrill whinny that surely was her song, if song she had, of love.

Old Turkeytrack studied the wind and the lay of the land. There was the pit he had labored at, now opened and filled with water that was rank with drowned prairie dogs and mice. Here was the new trail the animals were forced to make by the pit. He selected a sedgy clump near some smooth, grassy ground, and first firmly sunk the post, then dug a hole large enough to hide in, and spread his blanket in it. He shortened up the little mare's tether, till she could scarcely move; then on the ground between he spread his open lasso, tying the long end to the post, then covered the rope with dust and grass, and went into his hiding place.

About noon, after long waiting, the amorous whinny of the mare was answered from the high ground, away to the west, and there, black against the sky, was the famous Mustang.

Down he came at that long swinging gait, but grown crafty with much pursuit, he often stopped to gaze and whinny, and got answer that surely touched his heart. Nearer he came again to call, then took alarm, and paced all around in a great circle to try the wind for his foes, and seemed in doubt. The Angel whispered "Don't go." But the brown mare called again. He circled nearer still, and neighed once more, and got reply that seemed to quell all fears, and set his heart aglow.

Nearer still he pranced, till he touched Solly's nose with his own, and finding her as responsive as he well could wish, thrust aside all thought of danger, and abandoned himself to the delight of conquest, until, as he pranced around, his hind legs for a moment stood within the evil circle of the rope. One deft sharp twitch, the noose flew tight, and he was caught.

A snort of terror and a bound in the air gave Tom the chance to add the double hitch. The loop flashed up the line, and snake-like bound those mighty hoofs.

Terror lent speed and double strength for a moment, but the end of the rope was reached, and down he went a captive, a hopeless prisoner at last. Old Tom's ugly, little crooked form sprang from the pit to complete the mastering of the great glorious creature whose mighty strength had proved as nothing when matched with the wits of a little old man. With snorts and desperate bounds of awful force the great beast dashed and struggled to be free; but all in vain. The rope was strong.

The second lasso was deftly swung, and the forefeet caught, and then with a skillful move the feet were drawn together, and down went the raging Pacer to lie a moment later hog-tied and helpless on the ground. There he struggled till worn out, sobbing great convulsive sobs while tears ran down his cheeks.

Tom stood by and watched, but a strange revulsion of feeling came over the old cowpuncher. He trembled nervously from head to foot, as he had not done since he roped his first steer, and for a while could do nothing but gaze on his tremendous prisoner. But the feeling soon passed away. He saddled Delilah, and taking the second lasso, roped the great horse about the neck, and left the mare to hold the Stallion' head, while he put on the hobbles. This was soon done, and sure of him now old Bates was about to loose the ropes, but on a sudden thought he stopped. He had quite forgotten, and had come unprepared for something of importance. In Western law the Mustang was the property of the first man to mark him with his brand; how was this to be done with the nearest branding iron twenty miles away?

Old Tom went to his mare, took up her hoofs one at a time, and examined each shoe. Yes! One was a little loose; he pushed and pried it with the spade, and got it off. Buffalo chips and kindred fuel were plentiful about the plain, so a fire was quickly made, and he soon had one arm of the horseshoe red hot, then holding the other wrapped in his sock he rudely sketched on the left shoulder of the helpless mustang a turkey track, his brand, the first time really that it had ever been used. The Pacer shuddered as the hot iron seared his flesh, but it was quickly done, and the famous Mustang Stallion was a maverick no more.

Now all there was to do was to take him home. The ropes were loosed, the Mustang felt himself freed, thought he was free, and sprang to his feet only to fall as soon as he tried to take a stride. His forefeet were strongly tied together, his only possible gait a shuffling walk, or else a desperate labored bounding with feet so unnaturally held that within a few yards he was inevitably thrown each time he tried to break away. Tom on the light pony headed him off again and again, and by dint of driving, threatening, and maneuvering , contrived to force his foaming, crazy captive northward toward the Pinavetitos Canyon. But the wild horse would not drive, would not give in. With snorts of terror or of rage and maddest bounds, he tried and tried to get away. It was lone long cruel fight; his glossy sides were thick with dark foam, and the foam was stained with blood. Countless hard falls and exhaustion that a long day's chase was powerless to produce were telling on him; his straining bounds first this way and then that, were not now quite so strong, and the spray he snorted as he gasped was half a spray of blood. But his captor, relentless, masterful and cool, still forced him on. Down the slope toward the canyon they had come, every yard a fight, and now they were at the head of the draw that took the trail down to the only crossing of the canyon, the northmost limit of the Pacer's ancient range.

From this the first corral and ranch house were in sight. The man rejoiced, but the Mustang gathered his remaining strength for one more desperate dash. Up, up the grassy slope from the trail he went, defied the swinging, slashing rope and the gunshot fired in air, in vain attempt to turn his frenzied course. Up, up and on, above the sheerest cliff he dashed then sprang away into the vacant air, down—down—two hundred downward feet to fall, and land upon the rocks below, a lifeless wreck—but free.

Johnny Bear

eton and his wife Grace spent the summer of 1897 touring Yellowstone Park. During the trip they stayed one week at the Fountain Hotel which, although noted for its hot springs and baths, was more well known for its daily bear-feeding.

Each evening at six o'clock hotel employees would dump the hotel's garbage at a spot about one hundred yards from the building. Invariably, ten to fifteen bears would soon arrive for their daily meal. Most of them came so regularly to the garbage feeding that they were given names by the hotel staff.

While his wife went on sight-seeing excursions during their stay, Seton occupied his time sketching the bears and taking notes of their behavior. From these observations and through discussions with hotel employees, Seton became acquainted with Old Grumpy and her sickly, lame cub, Little Johnny. Several years later he wrote their story under the title of "Johnny Bear" that first appeared in *Scribner's Magazine* in December of 1900 and later as one of the stories in the book, *Lives of the Hunted,* published in 1901.

Johnny Bear

I

ohnny was a queer little bear cub that lived with Grumpy, his mother, in Yellowstone Park. They were among the many bears that found a desirable home in the country about the Fountain Hotel.

The steward of the hotel had ordered the kitchen garbage to be dumped in an open glade of the surrounding forest, thus providing, throughout the season, a daily feast for the bears, and their numbers have increased each year since the law of the land has made the Park a haven of refuge where no wild thing may be harmed. They have accepted man's peace offering, and many of them have become so well known to the hotel men that they have received names suggested by their looks or ways. Slim Jim was a very long legged thin black bear; Snuffy was a black bear that looked as though he had been singed; Fatty was a very fat, lazy bear that always lay down to eat; the Twins were two half-grown, ragged specimens that always came and went together. But Grumpy and Little Johnny were the best known of them all.

Grumpy was the biggest and fiercest of the black bears, and Johnny, apparently her only son, was a peculiarly tiresome little cub for he seemed never to cease

His whole appearance suggested dyspepsia.

either grumbling or whining. This probably meant that he was sick, for a healthy little bear does not grumble all the time, any more than a healthy a child. And indeed Johnny looked sick; he was the most miserable specimen in the Park. His whole appearance suggested dyspepsia; and this I quite understood when I saw the awful mixtures he would eat at the garbage heap. Anything at all that he fancied he would try. And his mother allowed him to do as he pleased; so, after all, it was chiefly her fault, for she should not have permitted such things.

Johnny had only three good legs, his coat was faded and mangy, his limbs were thin, and his ears and paunch were disproportionately large. Yet his mother thought the world of him. She was evidently convinced that he was a little beauty and the Prince of all Bears, so, of course, she quite spoiled him. She was always ready to get into trouble on his account, and he was always delighted to lead her there. Although such a wretched little failure, Johnny was far from being a fool, for he usually knew just what he wanted and how to get it, if teasing his mother could carry the point.

II

It was in the summer of 1897 that I made their acquaintance. I was in the Park to study the home life of the animals and had been told that in the woods near the Fountain Hotel I could see bears at any time, which, of course, I scarcely believed. But on stepping out of the back door five minutes after arriving, I came face to face with a large black bear and her two cubs.

I stopped short, not a little startled. The bears also stopped and sat up to look at me. Then Mother Bear made a curious short Koff Koff, and looked toward a near pine tree. The cubs seemed to know what she meant, for they ran to this tree and scrambled up like two little monkeys, and when safely aloft they sat like small boys, holding on with their hands, while their little black legs dangled in the air, and waited to see what was to happen down below.

The Mother Bear, still on her hind legs, came slowly toward me, and I began to feel very uncomfortable indeed, for she stood about six feet high in her stockings and had apparently never heard of the magical power of the human eye.

I had not even a stick to defend myself with, and when she gave a low growl, I was about to retreat to the Hotel, although previously assured that the bears have always kept their truce with man. However, just at this turning point the old one stopped, now but thirty feet away, and continued to survey me calmly. She seemed in doubt for a minute, but evidently made up her mind that, "although that human thing might be all right, she would take no chances for her little ones."

She looked up to her two hopefuls, and gave a peculiar whining, whereupon they, like obedient children, jumped, as at the word of command. There was nothing about them heavy or bear-like as commonly understood; lightly they swung from bough to bough till they dropped to the ground, and all went off together into the woods. I was much tickled by the prompt obedience of the little bears. As soon as their mother told them to do something they did it. They did not even offer a suggestion. But I also found out that there was a good reason for it, for had they not done as she had told them they would have got such a spanking as would have made them howl.

This was a delightful peep into bear home life, and would have been well worth coming for, if the insight had ended there. But my friends in the Hotel said that was not the best place for bears. I should go to the garbage heap, a quarter mile off in the forest. There, they said, I surely could see as many bears as I wished.

Early the next morning I went to this bears' banqueting hall in the pines and hid in the nearest bushes.

Before very long a large black bear came quietly out of the woods to the pile, and began turning over the garbage and feeding. He was very nervous, sitting up and looking about at each slight sound, or running away a few yards when startled by some trifle. At length he cocked his ears and galloped off into the pines, as another black bear appeared. He also behaved in the same timid manner, and at last ran away when I shook the bushes in trying to get a better view.

At the outset I myself had been very nervous, for, of course, no man is allowed to carry weapons in the Park; but the timidity of these bears reassured me, and thenceforth I forgot everything in the interest of seeing the great, shaggy creatures in their home life.

Soon I realized I could not get the close insight I wished from that bush, as it was seventy-five yards from the garbage pile. There was none nearer; so I did the only thing left to do; I went to the garbage pile itself, and, digging a hole big enough to hide in, remained there all day long, with cabbage stalks, old potato peelings, tomato cans, and carrion piled up in odorous heaps around me. Notwithstanding the opinions of countless flies, it was not an attractive place. Indeed, it was so unfragrant that at night, when I returned to the Hotel, I was not allowed to come in until after I had changed my clothes in the woods.

It had been a trying ordeal, but I surely did see bears that day. If I may reckon it a new bear each time one came, I must have seen over forty. But of course it was not, for the bears were coming and going. And yet I am certain of this; there were at least thirteen bears, for I had thirteen about me at one time.

All that day I used my sketch book and journal. Every bear that came was duly noted; and this process soon began to give the desired insight into their ways and personalities.

Many unobservant persons think and say that all Negroes or all Chinamen as well as all animals of a kind, look alike. But just as surely as each human being differs from the next, so surely each animal is different from its fellow; otherwise how would the old ones know their mates or the little ones their mother, as they certainly do? These feasting bears gave a good illustration of this, for each had its individuality; not two were quite alike in appearance or in character.

This curious fact also appeared: I could hear the woodpeckers pecking over one hundred yards away in the woods, as well as the chickadees chickadeeing, the blue jays blue jaying, and even the squirrels scampering across the leafy forest floor; and yet I did not hear one of those bears come. Their huge, padded feet always went down in exactly the right spot to break no stick, to rustle no leaf, showing how perfectly they had learned the art of going in silence through the woods.

III

All morning the bears came and went or wandered near my hiding place without discovering me; and, except for one or two brief quarrels, there was nothing very exciting to note. But about three in the afternoon it became more lively.

There were then four large bears feeding on the heap. In the middle was Fatty, sprawling at full length as he feasted, a picture of placid ursine content, puffing just a little at times as he strove to save himself the trouble of moving by darting out his tongue like a long red

serpent, farther and farther, in quest of the tidbits just beyond claw reach.

Behind him Slim Jim was puzzling over the anatomy and attributes of an ancient lobster. It was something outside his experience, but the principle, "In case of doubt take the trick," is well known in bear land and settled the difficulty.

The other two were clearing out fruit tins with marvelous dexterity. One supple paw would hold the tin while the long tongue would dart again and again through the narrow opening, avoiding the sharp edges, yet cleaning out the can to the last taste of its sweetness.

This pastoral scene lasted long enough to be sketched, but was ended abruptly. My eye caught a movement on the hill top whence all the bears had come, and out stalked a very large black bear with a tiny cub. It was Grumpy and Little Johnny.

The old bear stalked down the slope toward the feast, and Johnny hitched alongside, grumbling as he came, his mother watching him as solicitously as ever a hen did her single chick. When they were within thirty yards of the garbage heap, Grumpy turned to her son and said something which, judging from its effect, must have meant, "Johnny, my child, I think you had better stay here while I go and chase those fellows away."

Johnny obediently waited; but he wanted to see, so he sat up on his hind legs with eyes agog and ears acock.

Grumpy came striding along with dignity, uttering warning growls as she approached the four bears. They were too much engrossed to pay any heed

Old Grumpy stalked down the slope,
and Johnny hitched alongside.

to the fact that yet another one of them was coming, till Grumpy, now within fifteen feet, let out a succession of loud coughing sounds, and charged into them. Strange to say, they did not pretend to face her, but, as soon as they saw who it was, scattered and all fled for the woods.

Slim Jim could safely trust his heels, and the other two were not far behind; but poor Fatty, puffing hard and waddling like any other very fat creature, got along

But Johnny wanted to see.

but slowly, and, unluckily for him, he fled in the direction of Johnny, so that Grumpy overtook him in a few bounds and gave him a couple of sound slaps in the rear which, if they did not accelerate his pace, at least made him bawl, and saved him by changing his direction. Grumpy, now left alone in possession of the feast, turned toward her son and uttered the whining Er-r-r Er-r-r Er-r-r-r-r. Johnny responded eagerly. He came hoppity-hop on his three good legs as fast as he could, and, joining her on the garbage, they began to have such a good time that Johnny actually ceased grumbling.

He had evidently been there before now, for he seemed to know quite well the staple kinds of canned goods. One might almost have supposed that he had learned the brands, for a lobster tin had no charm for him as long as he could find those that once were filled with jam. Some of the tins gave him much trouble, as he was too greedy or too clumsy to escape being scratched by the sharp edges. One seductive fruit tin had a hole so large that he found he could force his head into it, and for a few minutes his joy was full as he licked into all the farthest corners. But when he tried to draw his head out, his sorrows began, for he found himself caught. He could not get out, and he scratched and screamed like any other spoiled child, giving his mother no end of concern, although she seemed not to know how to help him. When at length he got the tin off his head, he revenged himself by hammering it with his paws till it was perfectly flat.

A large syrup can made him happy for a long time. It had had a lid, so that the hole was round and smooth; but it was not big enough to admit his head, and he could not touch its riches with his tongue stretched out it longest. He soon hit on a plan, however. Putting in his little black arm, he churned it around, then drew out and licked it clean; and while he licked one he got the other one ready; and he did this again and again, until the can was as clean inside as when first it had left the factory.

A syrup-tin kept him happy for a long time.

A broken mouse trap seemed to puzzle him. He clutched it between his fore paws, their strong inturn being sympathetically reflected in his hind feet, and held it firmly for study. The cheesy smell about it was decidedly good, but the thing responded in such an uncanny way, when he slapped it, that he kept back a cry for help only by the exercise of unusual self control. After gravely inspecting it, with his head first on this side and then on that, and his lips puckered into a little tube, he submitted it to the same punishment as that meted out to the refractory fruit tin, and was rewarded by discovering a nice little bit of cheese in the very heart of the culprit.

Johnny had evidently never heard of ptomaine poisoning, for nothing came amiss. After the jams and fruits gave out he turned his attention to the lobster and sardine cans, and was not appalled by even the Army beef. His paunch grew quite balloon-like, and from much licking his arms looked thin and shiny, as though he was wearing black silk gloves.

IV

It occurred to me that I might now be in a really dangerous place. For it is one thing surprising a bear that has no family responsibilities, and another stirring up a bad-tempered old mother by frightening her cub.

"Supposing," I thought, "that cranky Little Johnny should wander over to this end of the garbage and find me in the hole; he will at once set up a squall, and his mother, of course, will think I am hurting him,

and, without giving me a chance to explain, may forget the rules of the Park and make things very unpleasant."

Luckily, all the jam pots were at Johnny's end; he stayed by them, and Grumpy stayed by him. At length he noticed that his mother had a better tin than any he could find, and as he ran whining to take it from her he chanced to glance away up the slope. There he saw something that made him sit up and utter a curious little Koff Koff Koff Koff Koff.

His mother turned quickly, and sat up to see "what the child was looking at." I followed their gaze, and there, oh horrors! was an enormous Grizzly bear. He was a monster; he looked like a fur-clad omnibus coming through the trees.

Johnny set up a whine at once and got behind his mother. She uttered a deep growl, and all her back hair stood on end. Mine did too, but I kept as still as possible.

With stately tread the Grizzly came on. His vast shoulders sliding along his sides, and his silvery robe swaying at each tread, like the trappings on an elephant, gave an impression of power that was appalling.

Johnny began to whine more loudly, and I fully sympathized with him now, though I did not join in. After a moment's hesitation Grumpy turned to her noisy cub

Johnny got behind his mother.

and said something that sounded to me like two or three short coughs - Koff Koff Koff. But I imagine that she really said, "My child, I think you had better get up that tree, while I go and drive the brute away."

At any rate, that was what Johnny did, and this what she set out to do. But Johnny had no notion of missing any fun. He wanted to see what was going to happen. So he did not rest contented where he was hidden in the thick branches of the pine, but combined safety with view by climbing to the topmost branch that would bear him, and there, sharp against the sky, he squirmed about and squealed aloud in his excitement. The branch was so small that it bent under his weight, swaying this way and that as he shifted about, and every moment I expected to see it snap off. If it had been broken when swaying my way, Johnny would certainly have fallen on me, and this would probably have resulted in bad feelings between myself and his mother; but the limb was tougher than it looked, or perhaps Johnny had had plenty of experience, for he neither lost his hold nor broke the branch.

Meanwhile, Grumpy stalked out to meet the Grizzly. She stood as high as she could and set all her bristles on end; then, growling and chopping her teeth, she faced him.

The Grizzly, so far as I could see, took no notice of her. He came striding toward the feast as though alone. But when Grumpy got within twelve feet of him she uttered a succession of short, coughy roars, and, charging, gave him a tremendous blow on the ear. The Grizzly was surprised; but he replied with a left-hander that knocked her over like a sack of hay.

Nothing daunted, but doubly furious, she jumped up and rushed at him.

Then they clinched and rolled over and over, whacking and pounding, snorting and growling, and making no end of dust and rumpus. But above all their noise I could clearly hear Little Johnny, yelling at the top of his voice, and evidently encouraging his mother to go right in and finish the Grizzly at once.

Why the Grizzly did not break her in two I could not understand. After a few minutes' struggle, during which I could see nothing but dust and dim flying legs, the two separated as by mutual consent,—perhaps the

Then they clinched.

regulation time was up,—and for a while they stood glaring at each other, Grumpy at least much winded.

The Grizzly would have dropped the matter right there. He did not wish to fight. He had no idea of troubling himself about Johnny. All he wanted was a quiet meal. But no! The moment he took one step toward the garbage pile, that is, as Grumpy thought, toward Johnny, she went at him again. But this time the Grizzly was ready for her. With one blow he knocked her off her feet and sent her crashing on to a huge upturned pine root. She was fairly staggered this time. The force of the blow, and the rude reception of the rooty antlers, seemed to take all the fight out of her. She scrambled over and tried to escape. But the Grizzly was mad now. He meant to punish her, and dashed around the root. For a minute they kept up a dodging chase about it; but Grumpy was quicker of foot, and somehow always managed to keep the root between herself and her foe, while Johnny, safe in

the tree, continued to take an intense and uproarious interest.

At length, seeing he could not catch her that way, the Grizzly sat up on his haunches; and while he doubtless was planning a new move, old Grumpy saw her chance, and making a dash, got away from the root and up to the top of the tree where Johnny was perched.

Johnny came down a little way to meet her, or perhaps so that the tree might not break off with the additional weight. Having photographed this interesting group from my hiding place, I thought I must get a closer picture at any price, and for the first time in the day's proceedings I jumped out of the hole and ran under the tree. This move proved a great mistake, for here the thick lower boughs came between, and I could see nothing at all of the bears at the top.

I was close to the trunk, and was peering about and seeking for a chance to use the camera, when old Grumpy began to come down, chopping her teeth and uttering her threatening cough at me. While I stood in doubt, I heard a voice far behind me calling:

"Say, Mister! You better look out; that ole B'ar is liable to hurt you."

I turned to see the cowboy of the Hotel on his horse. He had been riding after the cattle, and chanced to pass near just as events were moving quickly.

"Do you know these bears?" said I, as he rode up.

"Wall, I reckon I do," said he. "That there little one up top is Johnny; he's a little crank. An' the big un is Grumpy; she's a big crank. She's mighty onreliable

gen'relly, but she's always strictly ugly when Johnny hollers like that."

"I should much like to get her picture when she comes down," said I.

"Tell ye what I'll do: I'll stay by on the pony, an' if she goes to bother you I reckon I can keep her off," said the man.

He accordingly stood by as Grumpy slowly came down from branch to branch, growling and threatening. But when she neared the ground she kept on the far side of the trunk, and finally slipped down and ran into the woods, without the slightest pretense of carrying out any of her dreadful threats. Thus Johnny was again left alone. He climbed up to his old perch and resumed his monotonous whining:

Wah! Wah! Wah! ("Oh, dear! Oh, dear! Oh dear!")

I got the camera ready, and was arranging deliberately to take his picture in his favorite and peculiar attitude for threnodic song, when all at once he began craning his neck and yelling, as he had done during the fight.

I looked where his nose pointed, and here was the Grizzly coming on straight toward me—not charging, but striding along, as though he meant to come the whole distance.

I said to my cowboy friend, "Do you know this bear?"

He replied, "Wall! I reckon I do. That's the ole Grizzly. He's the biggest b'ar in the Park. He gen'relly minds his own business, but he ain't scared o' nothin'; an' today, ye see, he's been scrappin', so he's liable to be ugly."

"I would like to take his picture," said I, "and if you will help me, I am willing to take some chances on it."

"All right," said he, with a grin. "I'll stand by on the horse, an' if he charges you I'll charge him; an' I kin knock him down once, but I can't do it twice. You better have your tree picked out."

As there was only one tree to pick out, and that was the one that Johnny was in, the prospect was not alluring. I imagined myself scrambling up there next to Johnny, and then Johnny's mother coming up after me, with the Grizzly below to catch me when Grumpy should throw me down.

The Grizzly came on, and I snapped him at forty yards, then again at twenty yards; and still he came quietly toward me. I sat down on the garbage and made ready. Eighteen yards—sixteen yards—twelve yards—eight yards, and still he came, while the pitch of Johnny's protests kept rising proportionately. Finally at five yards he stopped, and swung his huge bearded head to one side, to see what was making the aggravating row in the tree top, giving me a profile view, and I snapped the camera. At the click he turned on me with a thunderous G-R-O-W-L! and I sat still and trembling, wondering if my last moment had come. For a second he glared at me, and I could note that little green electric lamp in each of his eyes. Then he slowly turned and picked up a large tomato can.

"Goodness!" I thought, "is he going to throw that at me? But he deliberately licked it out, dropped it, and took another, paying thenceforth no heed whatever either to me or to Johnny, evidently considering us equally beneath his notice.

I backed slowly and respectfully out of his royal presence, leaving him in possession of the garbage, while Johnny kept on caterwauling from his safety perch.

What became of Grumpy the rest of that day I do not know. Johnny, after bewailing for a time, realized that there was no sympathetic hearer of his cries, and therefore very sagaciously stopped them. Having no mother now to plan for him, he began to plan for himself, and at once proved that he was better stuff than he seemed. After watching, with a look of profound cunning on his little black face, and waiting till the Grizzly was some distance away, he silently slipped down behind the trunk, and, despite his three-leggedness, ran like a hare to the next tree, never stopping to breathe till he was on its topmost bough. For he was thoroughly convinced that the only object that the Grizzly had in life was to kill him, and he seemed quite aware that his enemy could not climb a tree.

Another long and safe survey of the Grizzly, who really paid no heed to him whatever, was followed by another dash for the next tree, varied occasionally by a cunning feint to mislead the foe. So he went dashing from tree to tree and climbing each to its very top, although it might be but ten feet from the last, till he disappeared in the woods. After, perhaps, ten minutes, his voice again came floating on the breeze, the habitual querulous whining which told me he had found his mother and had resumed his customary appeal to her sympathy.

VI

It is quite a common thing for bears to spank their cubs when they need it, and if Grumpy had disciplined Johnny this way, it would have saved them both a deal of worry.

Perhaps not a day passed that summer without Grumpy getting into trouble on Johnny's account. But of all these numerous occasions the most ignominious was shortly after the affair with the Grizzly.

I first heard the story from three bronzed mountaineers. As they were very sensitive about having their word doubted, and very good shots with the revolver, I believed every word they told me, especially when afterward fully endorsed by the Park authorities.

It seemed that of all the tinned goods on the pile the nearest to Johnny's taste were marked with a large purple plum. This conclusion he had arrived at only after most exhaustive study. The very odor of those plums in Johnny's nostrils was the equivalent of ecstasy. So when it came about one day that the cook of the Hotel baked a huge batch of plum tarts, the telltale wind took the story afar into the woods, where it was wafted by way of Johnny's nostrils to his very soul.

Of course, Johnny was whimpering at the time. His mother was busy "washing his face and combing his hair," so he had double cause for whimpering. But the smell of the tarts thrilled him; he jumped up, and

95

when his mother tried to hold him he squalled, and I am afraid—he bit her. She should have cuffed him, but she did not. She only gave a disapproving growl, and followed to see that he came to no harm.

With his little black nose in the wind, Johnny led straight for the kitchen. He took the precaution, however, of climbing from time to time to the very top of a pine tree lookout to take an observation, while Grumpy stayed below.

Thus they came close to the kitchen, and there, in the last tree, Johnny's courage as a leader gave out, so he remained aloft and expressed his hankering for tarts in a woe begone wail.

It is not likely that Grumpy knew exactly what her son was crying for. But it is sure that as soon as she showed an inclination to go back into the pines, Johnny protested in such an outrageous and heartrending screeching that his mother simply could not leave him, and he showed no sign of coming down to be led away.

Grumpy herself was fond of plum jam. The odor was now, of course, very strong and proportionately alluring; so Grumpy followed it somewhat cautiously up to the kitchen door.

There was nothing surprising about this. The rule of "live and let live" is so strictly enforced in the Park that the bears often come to the kitchen door for pickings, and on getting something, they go quietly back to the woods. Doubtless Johnny and Grumpy would each have gotten their tart but that a new factor appeared in the case.

That week the Hotel people had brought a new cat from the East. She was not much more than a kitten, but still had a litter of her own, and at the moment that Grumpy reached the door, the cat and her family were sunning themselves on the top step. Pussy opened her eyes to see this huge, shaggy monster towering above her.

The cat had never before seen a bear—she had not been there long enough; she did not know even what a bear was. She knew what a dog was, and here was a bigger, more awful bobtailed black dog than ever she had dreamed of coming right at her. Her first thought was to fly for her life. But her next was for the kittens. She must take care of them. She must at least cover their retreat. So, like a brave little mother, she braced herself on that door step, and spreading her back, her claws, her tail, and everything she had to spread, she screamed out at the bear an unmistakable order to, "STOP!"

The language must have been "cat," but the meaning was clear to the bear; for those who saw it maintain stoutly that Grumpy not only stopped, but she also conformed to the custom of the country and in token of surrender held up her hands.

However, the position she thus took made her so high that the cat seemed tiny in the distance below. Old Grumpy had faced a Grizzly once, and was she now to be held up by a miserable little spike-tailed skunk no bigger than a mouthful? She was ashamed of herself, especially when a wail from Johnny smote on her ear and reminded her of her plain duty, as well as supplied his usual moral support.

So she dropped down on her front feet to proceed.

Again the cat shrieked, "STOP!"

"Stop!" Shrieked the cat.

But Grumpy ignored the command. A scared mew from a kitten nerved the cat, and she launched her ultimatum, which ultimatum was herself. Eighteen sharp claws, a mouthful of keen teeth, had Pussy, and she worked them all with a desperate will when she landed on Grumpy's bare, bald, sensitive nose, just the spot of all where the bear could not stand it, and then worked backward to a point outside the sweep of Grumpy's claws. After one or two vain attempts to shake the spotted fury off, old Grumpy did just as most creatures would

Then pussy launched her ultimatum.

have done under the circumstances; she turned tail and bolted out of the enemy's country into her own woods.

But Puss's fighting blood was up. She was not content with repelling the enemy; she wanted to inflict a crushing defeat, to achieve an absolute and final rout. And however fast old Grumpy might go, it did not count, for the cat was still on top, working her teeth and claws like a little demon. Grumpy, always erratic, now became panic stricken. The trail of the pair was flecked with tufts of long black hair, and there was even blood shed. Honor surely was satisfied, but Pussy was not. Round and round they had gone in the mad race. Grumpy was frantic, absolutely humiliated, and ready to make any terms; but Pussy seemed deaf to her cough-like yelps, and no one knows how far the cat might have ridden that day had not Johnny unwittingly put a new idea into his mother's head by bawling in his best style from the top of his last tree, which tree Grumpy made for and scrambled up.

This was so clearly the enemy's country and in view of his reinforcements that the cat wisely decided to follow no farther. She jumped from the climbing bear to the ground, and then mounted sentry guard below, marching around with tail in the air, daring that bear to come down. Then the kittens came out and sat around, and enjoyed it all hugely. And the mountaineers assured me that the bears would have been kept up the tree till they were starved, had not the cook of the Hotel come out and called off his cat—although his statement was not among those vouched for by the officers of the Park.

VII

The last time I saw Johnny he was in the top of a tree, bewailing his unhappy lot as usual, while his mother was dashing about among the pines, "with a chip on her shoulder," seeking for some one—any one—that she could punish for Johnny's sake, provided, of course, that it was not a big Grizzly or a Mother Cat.

This was early in August, but there were not lacking symptoms of change in old Grumpy. She was always reckoned "onsartain," and her devotion to Johnny seemed subject to her characteristic. This perhaps accounted for the fact that when the end of the month was near, Johnny would sometimes spend half a day in the top of some tree, alone, miserable, and utterly unheeded.

The last chapter of his history came to pass after I had left the region. One day at grey dawn he was tagging along behind his mother as she prowled in the rear of the Hotel. A newly hired Irish girl was already astir in the kitchen. On looking out, she saw, as she thought, a calf where it should not be, and ran to shoo it away. That open kitchen door still held unmeasured terrors for Grumpy, and she ran in such alarm that Johnny caught the infection, and not being able to keep up with her, he made for the nearest tree, which unfortunately turned out to be a post, and soon—too soon—he arrived at its top, some seven feet from the ground, and there poured forth his woes on the chilly morning air, while Grumpy apparently felt justified in continuing her flight alone. When the girl came near and saw that she had treed some wild animal, she was as much frightened as her victim. But others of the kitchen staff appeared, and recognizing the vociferous Johnny, they decided to make him a prisoner.

A collar and chain were brought, and after a struggle, during which several of the men got well scratched, the collar was buckled on Johnny's neck and the chain made fast to the post.

When he found that he was held, Johnny was simply too mad to scream. He bit and scratched and tore till he was tired out. Then he lifted up his voice again to call his mother. She did appear once or twice in the distance, but could not make up her mind to face that cat, so disappeared, and Johnny was left to his fate.

He put in most of that day in alternate struggling and crying. Toward evening he was worn out, and glad to accept the meal that was brought by Norah, who felt herself called on to play mother, since she had chased his own mother away.

When night came it was very cold; but Johnny nearly froze at the top of the post before he would come down and accept the warm bed provided at the bottom.

During the day that followed, Grumpy came often to the garbage heap, but soon apparently succeeded in forgetting all about her son. He was daily tended by Norah, and received all his meals from her. He also received something else; for one day he scratched her when she brought his food, and she very properly spanked him till he squealed. For a few hours he sulked; he was not used to such treatment. But hunger subdued him, and thenceforth he held his new guardian in wholesome respect. She, too, began to take an interest in the poor motherless little wretch, and within a fortnight

Johnny showed signs of developing a new character. He was much less noisy. He still expressed his hunger in a whining Er-r-r Er-r-r Er-r-r, but he rarely squealed now, and his unruly outbursts entirely ceased.

By the third week of September the change was still more marked. Utterly abandoned by his own mother, all his interest had centered in Norah, and she had fed and spanked him into an exceedingly well-behaved little bear. Sometimes she would allow him a taste of freedom, and he then showed his bias by making, not for the woods, but for the kitchen where she was, and following her around on his hind legs. Here also he made the acquaintance of that dreadful cat; but Johnny had a powerful friend now, and Pussy finally became reconciled to the black, woolly interloper.

As the Hotel was to be closed in October, there was talk of turning Johnny loose or of sending him to the Washington Zoo; but Norah had claims that she would not forego.

When the frosty nights of late September came, Johnny had greatly improved in his manners, but he had also developed a bad cough. An examination of his lame leg had shown that the weakness was not in the foot, but much more deeply seated, perhaps in the hip, and that meant a feeble and tottering constitution.

He did not get fat, as do most bears in fall; indeed, he continued to fail. His little round belly shrank in, his cough became worse, and one morning he was found very sick and shivering in his bed by the post. Norah brought him indoors, where the warmth helped him so much that thenceforth he lived in the kitchen.

For a few days he seemed better, and his old time pleasure in seeing things revived. The great blazing fire in the range particularly appealed to him, and made him sit up in his old attitude when the opening of the door brought the wonder to view. After a week he lost interest

even in that, and drooped more and more each day. Finally not the most exciting noises or scenes around him could stir up his old fondness for seeing what was going on.

He coughed a good deal, too, and seemed wretched, except when in Norah's lap. Here he would cuddle up contentedly, and whine most miserably when she had to set him down again in his basket.

A few day before the closing of the Hotel, he refused his usual breakfast, and whined softly till Norah took him in her lap; then he feebly snuggled up to her, and his soft Er-r-r Er-r-r grew fainter, till it ceased. Half an hour later, when she laid him down to go about her work, Little Johnny had lost the last trace of his anxiety to see and know what was going on.

Tito

The Story of the Coyote that Learned How

Seton learned about a female coyote called Tito while in the Dakota Badlands at Howard Eaton's dude ranch in September of 1897. As with many of Seton's animal stories, the main part of the story about Tito was based on behavior he had observed, while the rest was derived from information he had gathered about other coyotes. Specifically, while trapping wolves in New Mexico in 1893, Seton had seen a coyote vomit strychnine poisoned meat. He used that fact in Tito's story in order to more fully illustrate typical coyote behavior.

Seton's story about Tito first appeared in *Scribner's Magazine* in August and September of 1900 and later as part of *Lives of the Hunted*.

Tito

The Story of the Coyote that Learned How

I

A raindrop may deflect a thunderbolt, or a hair may ruin an empire, as surely as a spider web once turned the history of Scotland; and if it had not been for one little pebble, this history of Tito might never have happened.

That pebble was lying on a trail in the Dakota Badlands, and one hot, dark night it lodged in the foot of a horse that was ridden by a tipsy cowboy. The man got off, as a matter of habit, to know what was laming his horse. But he left the reins on its neck instead of on the ground, and the horse, taking advantage of this technicality, ran off in the darkness. Then the cowboy, realizing that he was afoot, lay down in a hollow under some buffalo bushes and slept the loggish sleep of the befuddled.

The golden beams of the early summer sun were leaping from top to top of the wonderful Badland Buttes, when an old coyote might have been seen trotting homeward along the Garner's Creek Trail with a rabbit in her jaws to supply her family's breakfast.

Fierce war had for a long time been waged against the coyote kind by the cattlemen of Billings County. Traps, guns, poison, and hounds had reduced their number nearly to zero, and the few survivors had learned the bitter need of caution at every step. But the destructive ingenuity of man knew no bounds, and their numbers continued to dwindle.

The old coyote quit the trail very soon, for nothing that man has made is friendly. She skirted along a low ridge, then across a little hollow where grew a few buffalo bushes, and, after a careful sniff at a very stale human trail scent, she crossed another near ridge on whose sunny side was the home of her brood. Again she cautiously circled, peered about, and sniffed, but, finding no sign of danger, went down to the doorway and uttered a low woof-woof. Out of the den, beside a sagebrush, there poured a procession of little coyotes, merrily tumbling over one another. Then, barking little barks and growling little puppy growls, they fell upon the feast that their mother had brought, and gobbled and tussled while she looked on and enjoyed their joy.

Wolver Jake, the cowboy, had awakened from his chilly sleep about sunrise, in time to catch a glimpse of the coyote passing over the ridge. As soon as she was out of sight he got on his feet and went to the edge, there to witness the interesting scene of the family breakfasting and frisking about within a few yards of him, utterly unconscious of any danger.

But the only appeal the scene had to him lay in the fact that the county had set a price on every one of these coyotes' lives. So he got out his big .45 Navy revolver, and notwithstanding his shaky condition, he managed somehow to get a sight on the mother as she was caressing one of the little ones that had finished its breakfast, and shot her dead on the spot.

The terrified cubs fled into the den, and Jake, failing to kill another with his revolver, came forward, blocked up the hole with stones, and leaving the seven little prisoners quaking at the far end, set off on foot for the nearest ranch, cursing his faithless horse as he went.

In the afternoon he returned with his pard and tools for digging. The little ones had cowered all day in the darkened hole, wondering why their mother did not come to feed them, wondering at the darkness and the change. But late that day they heard sounds at the door. Then light was again let in. Some of the less cautious young ones ran forward to meet their mother, but their mother was not there—only two great rough brutes that began tearing open their home.

After an hour or more the diggers came to the end of the den, and here were the woolly, bright-eyed little ones, all huddled in a pile at the farthest corner. Their innocent puppy faces and ways were not noticed by the huge enemy. One by one they were seized. A sharp blow, and each quivering, limp form was thrown into a sack to be carried to the nearest magistrate who was empowered to pay the bounties.

Even at this age there was a certain individuality of character among the puppies. Some of them squealed and some of them growled when dragged out to die. One or two tried to bite. The one that had been slowest to comprehend the danger had been the last to retreat, and so was on top of the pile, and therefore the first killed. The one that had first realized the peril had retreated first, and now crouched at the bottom of the pile. Coolly and remorselessly the others were killed one by one, and then this prudent little puppy was seen to be the last of the family. It lay perfectly still, even when touched, its eyes being half closed, as guided by instinct, it tried to "play possum." One of the men picked it up. It neither squealed nor resisted. Then Jake, realizing ever the importance of "standing in with the boss," said, "Say, let's keep that 'un for the children." So the last of the family was thrown alive into the same bag with its dead brothers, and, bruised and frightened, lay there very still, understanding nothing, knowing only that after a long time of great noise and cruel jolting it was again half strangled by the grip on its neck and dragged out, where were a lot of creatures like the diggers.

These were really the inhabitants of the Chimney-Pot Ranch, whose brand is the Broad Arrow; and among them were the children for whom the cub had been brought. The boss had no difficulty in getting Jake to accept the dollar that cub coyote would have brought in bounty money, and his present was turned over to the children. In answer to their question, "What is it?" a Mexican cowhand present said it was a coyotito,—that is , a "little coyote,"—and this, afterward shortened to "Tito," became the captive's name.

II

Tito was a pretty little creature, with woolly body, a puppy-like expression, and a head that was singularly broad between the ears.

But, as a children's pet, she—for it proved to be a female—was not a success. She was distant and distrustful. She ate her food and seemed healthy, but never responded to friendly advances; never even learned to come out of the box when called. This probably was due to the fact that the kindness of the small children was offset by the roughness of the men and boys, who did not hesitate to drag her out by the chain when they wished to see her. On these occasions she would suffer in silence, playing possum, shamming dead, for she seemed to know that that was the best thing to do. But as soon as released she would once more retire into the darkest corner of her box and watch her tormentors with eyes that, at the proper angle, showed a telling glint of green.

Among the children of the ranchmen was a thirteen-year-old boy. The fact that he grew up to be like his father, a kind, strong, and thoughtful man, did not prevent him being, at this age, a shameless little brute.

Like all boys in that country, he practiced lasso-throwing, with a view to being a cowboy. Posts and stumps are uninteresting things to catch. His little brothers and sisters were under special protection of the Home Government. The dogs ran far away whenever they saw him coming with the rope in his hands. So he must needs practice on the unfortunate Coyotito. She soon learned that her only hope for peace was to hide in the kennel, or, if thrown at when outside, to dodge the rope by lying as flat as possible on the ground. Thus

Coyotito, the captive

Lincoln unwittingly taught the coyote the dangers and limitations of a rope, and so he proved a blessing in disguise—a very perfect disguise. When the coyote had thoroughly learned how to baffle the lasso, the boy terror devised a new amusement. He got a large trap of the kind known as "fox-size." This he set in the dust as he had seen Jake set a wolf trap, close to the kennel, and over it he scattered scraps of meat, in the most approved style for wolf trapping. After a while Tito, drawn by the smell of the meat, came hungrily sneaking out toward it, and almost immediately was caught in the trap by one foot. The boy terror was watching from a near hiding place. He gave a wild Indian whoop of delight, then rushed forward to drag the coyote out of the box into which she had retreated. After some more delightful thrills of excitement and struggle he got his lasso on Tito's body, and, helped by a younger brother, a most promising pupil, he succeeded in setting the coyote free from the trap before the grown ups had discovered his amusement. One or two experiences like this taught her a mortal terror of traps. She soon learned the smell of the steel, and could detect and avoid it, no matter how cleverly Master Lincoln might bury it in the dust, while the younger brother screened the operation from the intended victim by holding his coat over the door of Tito's kennel.

One day the fastening of her chain gave way, and Tito went off in an uncertain fashion, trailing her chain behind her. But she was seen by one of the men, who fired a charge of bird shot at her. The burning, stinging, and surprise of it all caused her to retreat to the one place she knew, her own kennel. The chain was fastened again, and Tito added to her ideas this, a horror of guns and the smell of gunpowder; and this also, that the one safety from them was to "lay low."

There were yet other rude experiences in store for the captive.

Poisoning wolves was a topic of daily talk at the ranch, so it was not surprising that Lincoln should privately experiment on Coyotito. The deadly strychnine was too well guarded to be available. So Lincoln hid some Rough on Rats in a piece of meat, threw it to the captive, and sat by to watch, as blithe and conscience-clear as any professor of chemistry trying a new combination.

Tito smelled the meat—everything had to be passed on by her nose. Her nose was in doubt. There was a good smell of meat, a familiar but unpleasant smell of human hands, and a strange new odor, but not the odor of the trap; so she bolted the morsel. Within a few minutes she began to have fearful pains in her stomach, followed by cramps. Now in all the wolf tribe there is the instinctive habit to throw up anything that disagrees with them, and after a minute or two of suffering the Coyote sought relief in this way; and to make it doubly sure she hastily gobbled some blades of grass, and in less than an hour was quite well again.

Lincoln had put in poison enough for a dozen coyotes. Had he put in less she could not have felt the pang till too late, but she recovered and never forgot that peculiar smell that means such awful after pains. More than that, she was ready thenceforth to fly at once to the herbal cure that Nature had everywhere provided. An instinct of this kind grows quickly, once followed. It had taken minutes of suffering in the first place to drive her to the easement. Thenceforth, having learned, it was her first thought on feeling pain. The little miscreant did indeed succeed in having her swallow another bait with a small dose of poison, but she knew what to do now and had almost no suffering.

Later on, a relative sent Lincoln a Bull terrier, and the new combination was a fresh source of spectacular interest for the boy, and of tribulation for the coyote. It all emphasized for her that old idea to "lay low"—that is, to be quiet, unobtrusive, and hide when danger is in sight. The grownups of the household at length forbade these persecutions, and the terrier was kept away from the little yard where the coyote was chained up.

It must not be supposed that, in all this, Tito was a sweet, innocent victim. She had learned to bite. She had caught and killed several chickens by shamming sleep while they ventured to forage within the radius of her chain. And she had an inborn hankering to sing a morning and evening hymn, which procured for her many beatings. But she learned to shut up, the moment her opening notes were followed by a rattle of doors or windows, for these sounds of human  nearness had frequently been followed by a bang and a charge of bird shot, which somehow did no serious harm, though it severely stung her hide. And these experiences all helped to deepen her terror of guns and of those who used them. The object of the musical outpourings was not clear. They happened usually at dawn or dusk, but sometimes a loud noise at high noon would set her going. The song consisted of a volley of short barks, mixed with doleful squalls that never failed to set the dogs astir in a responsive uproar, and once or twice had begotten a far away answer from some wild coyote in the hills.

There was one little trick that she developed which was purely instinctive—that is, an inherited habit. In the back end of her kennel she had a little cache of bones, and knew exactly where one or two lumps of unsavory meat were buried within the radius of her chain, for a time of famine which never came. If any one approached these hidden treasures, she watched with anxious eyes, but made no other demonstration. If she saw that the meddler knew the exact place, she took an early opportunity to secrete them elsewhere.

After a year of this life Tito had grown to full size, and had learned many things that her wild kinsmen could not have learned without losing their lives in doing it. She knew and feared traps. She had learned to avoid poison baits, and knew what to do at once if, by some mistake, she should take one. She knew what guns were. She had learned to cut her morning and evening song very short. She had some acquaintance with dogs, enough to make her hate and distrust them all. But, above all, she had this idea: whenever danger was near, the very best move possible was to lay low, be very quiet, do nothing to attract notice. Perhaps the little brain that looked out of those changing yellow eyes was the storehouse of much other knowledge about men, but what it was did not appear.

The coyote was fully grown when the boss of the outfit bought a couple of thoroughbred greyhounds, wonderful runners, to see whether he could not entirely extirpate the remnant of the coyotes that still destroyed occasional sheep and calves on the range, and at the same time find amusement in the sport. He was tired of seeing that coyote in the yard; so, deciding to use her for training the dogs, he had her roughly thrown into a bag, then carried a quarter of a mile away and dumped out. At the same time the greyhounds were slipped and chivvied on. Away they went bounding at their matchless pace that nothing else on four legs could equal and away went the coyote, frightened by the noise of the men, frightened even to find herself free. Her quarter mile start quickly shrank to one hundred yards, the one hundred to fifty, and on sped the flying dogs. Clearly there was no chance for her. On and nearer they came. In another minute she would have been stretched out—not a doubt of it. But on a sudden she stopped, turned, and walked toward the dogs with her tail serenely waving in the air and a friendly cock to her ears. Greyhounds are peculiar dogs. Anything that runs away, they are going to catch and kill if they can. Anything that is calmly facing them becomes at once a noncombatant. They bounded over and past the coyote before they could curb their own impetuosity, and returned completely nonplused. Possibly they recognized the coyote of the house yard as she stood there wagging her tail. The ranchmen were nonplused too. Every one was utterly taken aback, had a sense of failure, and the real victor in the situation was felt to be the audacious little coyote.

The greyhounds refused to attack an animal that wagged its tail and would not run; and the men, on seeing that the coyote could walk far enough away to avoid being caught by hand, took their ropes, and soon made her a prisoner once more.

The next day they decided to try again, but this time they added the white Bull terrier to the chasers. The coyote did as before. The greyhounds declined to be party to any attack on such a mild and friendly acquaintance. But the Bull terrier, who came puffing and panting on the scene three minutes later, had no such scruples. He was not so tall, but he was heavier than the coyote, and seizing her by her wool-protected neck, he shook her till, in a surprising short time, she lay limp and lifeless, at which all the men seemed pleased, and congratulated the terrier, while the greyhounds pottered around in restless perplexity.

A stranger in the party, a newly arrived Englishman, asked if he might have the brush—the tail, he explained—and on being told to help himself, he picked up the victim by the tail, and with one awkward chop of his knife he cut it off at the middle, and the coyote dropped, but gave a shrill yelp of pain. She was not dead, only playing possum, and now she leaped up and vanished into a nearby thicket of cactus and sage.

With greyhounds, a running animal is the signal for a run, so the two long-legged dogs and the white, broad-chested dog dashed after the coyote. But right across their path, by happy chance, there flashed a brown streak ridden by a snowy powder-puff, the visible but evanescent sign for cottontail rabbit. The coyote was not in sight now. The rabbit was, so the greyhounds dashed after the cottontail, who took advantage of a prairie dog's hole to seek safety in the bosom of Mother Earth, and the coyote made good her escape.

She had been a good deal jarred by the rude treatment of the terrier, and her mutilated tail gave her some pain. But otherwise she was all right, and she loped lightly away, keeping out of sight in the hollows, and so escaped among the fantastic buttes of the Badlands, to be eventually the founder of a new life among the coyotes of the Little Missouri.

Moses was preserved by the Egyptians till he had outlived the dangerous period, and learned from them wisdom enough to be the savior of his people against those same Egyptians. So the bobtailed coyote was not only saved by man and carried over the dangerous period of puppy hood; she was also unwittingly taught by him how to baffle the traps, poisons, lassos, guns, and dogs that had so long waged a war of extermination against her race.

III

Thus Tito escaped from man, and for the first time found herself face to face with the whole problem of life; for now she had her own living to get.

A wild animal has three sources of wisdom:

First, the experience of its ancestors, in the form of instinct, which is inborn learning, hammered into the race by ages of selection and tribulation. This is the most important to begin with, because it guards him from the moment he is born.

Second, the experience of his parents and comrades, learned chiefly by example. This becomes most important as soon as the young can run.

Third, the personal experience of the animal itself. This grows in importance as the animal ages.

The weakness of the first is its fixity; it cannot change to meet quickly changing conditions. The weakness of the second is the animal's inability freely to exchange ideas by language. The weakness of the third is the danger in acquiring it. But the three together are a strong arch.

Now, Tito was in a new case. Perhaps never before had a coyote faced life with unusual advantages in the third kind of knowledge, none at all in the second, and with the first dormant. She traveled rapidly away from the ranchmen, keeping out of sight, and sitting down once in a while to lick her wounded tail. She came at last to a prairie dog town. Many of the inhabitants were out, and they barked at the intruder, but all dodged down as soon as she came near. Her instinct taught her to try and catch one, but she ran about in vain for some time, and then gave it up. She would have gone hungry that night but that she found a couple of mice in the long grass by the river. Her mother had not taught her to hunt, but her instinct did, and the accident that she had an unusual brain made her profit very quickly by her experience.

In the days that followed she quickly learned how to make a living; for mice, ground squirrels, prairie dogs, rabbits, and lizards were abundant, and many of these could be captured in open chase. But open chase, and sneaking as near as possible before beginning the open chase, lead naturally to stalking for a final spring. And before the moon had changed the coyote had learned how to make a comfortable living.

Once or twice she saw the men with the greyhounds coming her way. Most coyotes would, perhaps, have barked in bravado, or would have gone up to some high place whence they could watch the enemy; but Tito did no such foolish thing. Had she run, her moving form would have caught the eyes of the dogs, and then nothing could have saved her. She dropped where she was, and lay flat until the danger had passed. Thus her ranch training to lay low began to stand her in good stead, and so it came about that her weakness was her strength. The coyote kind had so long been famous for their speed, had so long learned to trust in their legs, that they never dreamed of a creature that could run them down. They were accustomed to play with their pursuers, and so rarely bestirred themselves to run from greyhounds, till it was too late. But Tito, brought up at the end of a chain, was a poor runner. She had no reason to trust her legs. She rather trusted her wits, and so lived.

During that summer she stayed about the Little Missouri, learning the tricks of small game hunting that she should have learned before she shed her milk teeth, and gaining in strength and speed. She kept far away from all the ranches, and always hid on seeing a man or a strange beast, and so passed the summer alone. During the daytime she was not lonely, but when the sun went down she would feel the impulse to sing that wild song of the West which means so much to the coyotes.

It is not the invention of an individual nor of the present, but was slowly built out of the feelings of all coyotes in all ages. It expresses their nature and the Plains

that made their nature. When one begins it, it takes hold of the rest, as the fife and drum do with soldiers, or the ki-yi war song with Indian braves. They respond to it as a bell glass does to a certain note the moment that note is struck, ignoring other sounds. So the coyote, no matter how brought up, must vibrate at the night song of the Plains, for it touches something in himself.

They sing it after sundown, when it becomes the rallying cry of their race and the friendly call to a neighbor; and they sing it as one boy in the woods holloas to another to say, "All's well! Here am I. Where are you?" A form of it they sing to the rising moon, for this is the time for good hunting to begin. They sing when they see a new camp fire, for the same reason that a dog barks at a stranger. Yet another weird chant they have for the dawning before they steal quietly away from the offing of the camp—a wild, weird, squalling refrain: Wow-wow-wow-wow-wow-w-o-o-o-o-o-w, again and again; and doubtless with many another change that man cannot distinguish any more than the coyote can distinguish the words in the cowboy's anathemas.

Tito instinctively uttered her music at the proper times. But sad experiences had taught her to cut it short and keep it low. Once or twice she had got a far away reply from one of her own race, whereupon she had quickly ceased and timidly quit the neighborhood.

One day, when on the Upper Garner's Creek, she found the trail where a piece of meat had been dragged along. It was a singularly inviting odor, and she followed it, partly out of curiosity. Presently she came on a piece of the meat itself. She was hungry; she was always hungry now. It was tempting, and although it had a peculiar odor, she swallowed it. Within a few minutes she felt a terrific pain.. The memory of the poisoned meat the boy had given her, was fresh. With trembling, foaming jaws she seized some blades of grass, and her stomach threw off the meat; but she fell in convulsions on the ground.

The trail of meat dragged along and the poison baits had been laid the day before by Wolver Jake. This morning he was riding the drag, and on coming up from the draw he saw, far ahead, the coyote struggling. He knew, of course, that it was poisoned, and rode quickly up; but the convulsions passed as he neared. By a mighty effort, at the sound of the horse's hoofs the coyote arose to her front feet. Jake drew his revolver and fired, but the only effect was fully to alarm her. She tried to run, but her hind legs were paralyzed. She put forth all her strength, dragging her hind legs. Now, when the poison was no longer in the stomach, will power could do a great deal. Had she been allowed to lie down then she would have been dead in five minutes; but the revolver shots and the man coming stirred her to strenuous action. Madly she struggled again and again to get her hind legs to work. All the force of desperate intent she brought to bear. It was like putting forth tenfold power to force the nervous fluids through their blocked up channels as she dragged herself with marvelous speed downhill. What is nerve but will? The dead wires of her legs were hot with this fresh power, multiplied, injected, blasted into

them. They had to give in. She felt them thrill with life again. Each wild shot from the gun lent vital help. Another fierce attempt, and one hind leg obeyed the call to duty. A few more bounds, and the other, too, fell in. Then lightly she loped away among the broken buttes, defying the agonizing grip that still kept on inside.

Had Jake held off then she would yet have laid down and died; but he followed, and fired and fired, till in another mile she bounded free from pain, saved from her enemy by himself. He had compelled her to take the only cure, so she escaped.

And these were the ideas that she harvested that day; that curious smell on the meat stands for mortal agony. Let it alone! And she never forgot it; thenceforth she knew strychnine.

Fortunately, dogs, traps, and strychnine do not wage war at once, for the dogs are as apt to be caught or poisoned as the coyotes. Had there been a single dog in the hunt that day Tito's history would have ended.

IV

When the weather grew cooler toward the end of autumn Tito had gone far toward repairing the defects in her early training. She was more like an ordinary coyote in her habits now, and she was more disposed to sing the sundown song.

One night, when she got a response, she yielded to the impulse again to call, and soon afterward a large, dark coyote appeared. The fact that he was there at all was a guarantee of unusual gifts, for the war against race was waged relentlessly by the cattlemen. He approached with caution. Tito's mane bristled with mixed feelings at the sight of one of her own kind. She crouched flat on the ground and waited. The newcomer came stiffly forward, nosing the wind; then up the wind nearly to her. Then he walked around so that she should wind him, and raising his tail, gently waved it. The first acts meant armed neutrality, but the last was a distinctly friendly signal. Then he approached, and she rose up suddenly and stood as high as she could to be smelled. Then she wagged the stump of her tail, and they considered themselves acquainted.

The newcomer was a very large coyote, half as tall again as Tito, and the dark patch on his shoulders was so large and black that the cowboys, when they came to know him, called him Saddleback. From that time these two continued more or less together. They were not always close together, often were miles apart during the day, but toward night one or the other would get on some high open place and sing the loud, Yap-yap-yap-

They considered themselves acquainted.

yow-wow-wow-wow-wow, and they would gather for some foray at hand.

The physical advantages were with Saddleback, but the greater cunning was Tito's, so that she in time became the leader. Before a month, a third coyote had appeared on the scene and become a member of this loose bound fraternity, and later two more appeared. Nothing succeeds like success. The little bobtailed coyote had had rare advantages of training just where the others were lacking; she knew the devices of man. She could not tell about these in words, but she could by the aid of a few signs and a great deal of example. It soon became evident that her methods of hunting were successful, whereas, when they went without her, they often had hard luck. A man at Boxelder Ranch had twenty sheep. The rules of the country did not allow any one to own more, as this was a cattle range. The sheep were guarded by a large and fierce collie. One day in winter two of the coyotes tried to raid this flock by a bold dash, and all they got was a mauling from the collie. A few days later the band returned at dusk. Just how Tito arranged it, man cannot tell. We can only guess how she taught them their parts, but we know that she surely did. The coyotes hid in the willows. Then Saddleback, the bold and swift, walked openly toward the sheep and barked a loud defiance. The collie jumped up with bristling mane and furious growl, then seeing the foe, dashed straight at him. Now was the time for the steady nerve and the unfailing limbs. Saddleback let the dog come near enough almost to catch him, and so beguiled him far and away into the woods, while the other coyotes, led by Tito, stampeded the sheep in twenty directions; then following the farthest, they killed several and left them in the snow.

In the gloom of descending night the dog and
his master labored till they had gathered the bleating

survivors; but next morning they found that four had been driven far away and killed, and the coyotes had had a banquet royal.

The shepherd poisoned the carcasses and left them. Next night the coyotes returned. Tito sniffed the now frozen meat, detected the poison, gave a warning growl, and scattered filth over the meat, so that none of the band should touch it. One, however, who was fast and foolish, persisted in feeding in spite of Tito's warning, and when they came away he was lying poisoned and dead in the snow.

V

Jake now heard on all sides that the coyotes were getting worse. So he set to work with many traps and much poison to destroy those on the Garner's Creek, and every little while he would go with the hounds and scour the Little Missouri south and east of the Chimney Pot Ranch; for it was understood that he must never run the dogs in country where traps and poison were laid. He worked in his erratic way all winter, and certainly did have some success. He killed a couple of gray wolves, said to be the last of their race, and several coyotes, some of which, no doubt, were of the Bobtailed pack, which thereby lost those members which were lacking in wisdom.

Yet that winter was marked by a series of coyote raids and exploits; and usually the track in the snow or the testimony of eyewitnesses told that the master spirit of it all was a little bobtailed coyote.

One of these adventures was the cause of much talk. The coyote challenge sounded close to the Chimney Pot Ranch after sundown. A dozen dogs responded with the usual clamor. But only the Bull terrier dashed away toward the place whence the coyotes had called, for the reason that he only was loose. His chase was fruitless, and he came back growling. Twenty minutes later there was another coyote yell close at hand. Off dashed the terrier as before. In a minute his excited yapping told that the had sighted his game and was in full chase. Away he went, furiously barking, until his voice was lost afar, and nevermore was heard. In the morning the men read in the snow the tale of the night. The first cry of the coyotes was to find out if all the dogs were loose; then, having found that only one was free, they laid a plan. Five coyotes hid along the side of the trail; one went forward and called till it had decoyed the rash terrier, and then led him right into the ambush. What chance had he with six? They tore him limb from limb, and devoured him, too, at the very spot where once he had worried Coyotito. And next morning, when the men came, they saw by the signs that the whole thing had been planned, and that the leader whose cunning had made it a success was a little bobtailed coyote.

The men were angry, and Lincoln was furious; but Jake remarked, "Well, I guess that Bobtail came back and got even with that terrier."

VI

When spring was near, the annual love season of the coyotes came on. Saddleback and Tito had been together merely as companions all winter, but now a new feeling was born. There was not much courting. Saddleback simply showed his teeth to possible rivals. There was no ceremony. They had been friends for months, and now, in the light of the new feeling, they naturally took to each other and were mated. Coyotes do not give each other names as do mankind, but have one sound like a growl and short howl, which stands for mate or husband or wife. This they use in calling to each other, and it is by recognizing the tone of the voice that they know who is calling.

The loose rambling brotherhood of the coyotes was broken up now, for the others also paired off, and since the returning warm weather was bringing out the prairie dogs and small game, there was less need to combine for hunting. Ordinarily coyotes do not sleep in dens or in any fixed place. They move about all night while it is cool, then during the daytime they get a few hours sleep in the sun, on some quiet hillside that also gives a chance to watch out. But the mating season changes this habit somewhat.

As the weather grew warm Tito and Saddleback set about preparing a den for the expected family. In a warm little hollow, an old badger abode was cleaned out, enlarged, and deepened. A quantity of leaves and grass was carried into it and arranged in a comfortable nest. The place selected for it was a dry, sunny nook among the hills, half a mile west of the Little Missouri. Thirty yards from it was a ridge which commanded a wide view of the grassy slopes and cottonwood groves by the river. Men would have called the spot very beautiful, but it is

Their evening song.

tolerably certain that that side of it never touched the coyotes at all.

Tito began to be much preoccupied with her impending duties. She stayed quietly in the neighborhood of the den, and lived on such food as Saddleback brought her, or she herself could easily catch, and also on the little stores that she had buried at other times. She knew every prairie dog town in the region, as well as all the best places for mice and rabbits.

Not far from the den was the very dog town that first she had crossed the day she had gained her liberty and lost her tail. If she were capable of such retrospect, she must have laughed to herself to think what a fool she was then. The change in her methods was now shown. Somewhat removed from the others, a prairie dog had made his den in the most approved style, and now when Tito peered over he was feeding on the grass ten yards from his own door. A prairie dog away from the others is, of course, easier to catch than one in the middle of the town, for he had but one pair of eyes to guard him; so Tito set about stalking this one. How was she to do it when there was no cover, nothing but short grass and a few low weeds? The white bear knows how to approach the seal on the flat ice, and the Indian how to get within striking distance of the grazing deer. Tito knew how to do the same trick, and although one of the town owls flew over with a warning chuckle, Tito set about her plans. A prairie dog cannot see well unless he is sitting up on his hind leg; his eyes are of little use when he is nosing in the grass; and Tito knew this. Further, a yellowish-grey animal on a yellowish-grey landscape is invisible till it moves. Tito seemed to know that. So, without any attempt to crawl or hide, she walked gently upwind toward the prairie dog. Upwind, not in order to prevent the prairie dog smelling her, but so that she could smell him, which came to the same thing. As soon as the

Fair game.

prairie dog sat up with some food in his hand she froze into a statue. As soon as he dropped again to nose in the grass, she walked steadily nearer, watching his every move so that she might be motionless each time he sat up to see what his distant brothers were barking at. Once or twice he seemed alarmed by the calls of his friends, but he saw nothing and resumed his feeding. She soon cut the fifty yards down to ten, and the ten to five, and still was undiscovered. Then, when again the prairie dog dropped down to seek more fodder, she made a quick dash, and bore him off kicking and squealing. Thus does the angel of the pruning knife lop off those that are heedless and foolishly indifferent to the advantages of society.

VII

Tito had many adventures in which she did not come out so well. Once she nearly caught an antelope fawn, but the hunt was spoiled by the sudden appearance of the mother, who gave Tito a stinging blow on the side of the head and ended her hunt for that day. She never again made that mistake—she had sense. Once or twice she had to jump to escape the strike of a rattlesnake. Several times she had been fired at by hunters with long range rifles. And more and more she had to look out for the terrible grey wolves. The grey wolf, of course, is much larger and stronger than the coyote, but the coyote has the advantage of speed, and can always escape in the open. All it must beware of is being caught in a corner. Usually when a grey wolf howls the coyotes go quietly about their business elsewhere.

Tito had a curious fad, occasionally seen among the wolves and coyotes, of carrying in her mouth, for miles, such things as seemed to be interesting and yet were not tempting as eatables. Many a time had she trotted a mile or two with an old buffalo horn or a cast off shoe, only to drop it when something else attracted her attention. The cowboys who remark these things have various odd explanations to offer: one, that it is done to stretch the jaws, or keep them in practice, just as a man in training carries weights. Coyotes have, in common with dogs and wolves, the habit of calling at certain stations along their line of travel, to leave a record of their visit. These stations may be a stone, a tree, a post, or an old buffalo skull, and the coyote calling there can learn, by the odor and track of the last comer, just who the caller was, whence he came, and whither he went. The whole country is marked out by these intelligence depots. Now it often happens that a coyote that has not much else to do will carry a dry bone or some other useless object in its mouth, but sighting the signal post, will go toward it to get the news, lay down the bone, and afterward forget to take it along, so that the signal posts in time become further marked with a curious collection of odds and ends.

This singular habit was the cause of a disaster to the Chimney Pot wolf hounds, and a corresponding advantage to the coyotes in the war. Jake had laid a line of poison baits on the western bluffs. Tito knew what they were, and spurned them as usual; but finding more later, she gathered up three or four and crossed the Little Missouri toward the ranch house. This she circled at a safe distance; but when something made the pack of dogs break out into clamor, Tito dropped the baits, and next day, when the dogs were taken out for exercise, they found and devoured these scraps of meat, so that in ten minutes there were four hundred dollars' worth of greyhounds lying dead. This led to an edict against poisoning in that district, and thus was a great boon to the coyotes.

Tito quickly learned that not only each kind of game must be hunted in a special way, but different ones of each kind may require quite different treatment. The prairie dog with the outlying den was really an easy prey, but the town was quite compact now that he was gone. Near the center of it was a fine, big, fat prairie dog, a perfect Alderman, that she had made several vain attempts to capture. On one occasion she had crawled almost within leaping distance, when the angry buzz of a rattlesnake just ahead warned her that she was in danger. Not that the rattler cared anything about the prairie dog, but he did not wish to be disturbed; and Tito, who had an instinctive fear of the snake, was forced to abandon the hunt. The open stalk proved an utter failure with the Alderman, for the situation of his den made every dog in the town his sentinel; but he  was too good to lose, and Tito waited until circumstances made a new plan.

All coyotes have a trick of watching from a high lookout whatever passes along the roads. After it has passed they go down and examine its track. Tito had this habit, except that she was always careful to keep out of sight herself.

One day a wagon passed from the town to the southward. Tito lay low and watched it. Something dropped on the road. When the wagon was out of sight Tito sneaked down, first to smell the trail as a matter of habit, second to see what it was that had dropped. The object was really an apple, but Tito saw only an unattractive round green thing like a cactus leaf without spines, and of a peculiar smell. She snuffed it, spurned it, and was about to pass on; but the sun shone on it so brightly, and it rolled so curiously when she pawed, that

she picked it up in a mechanical way and trotted back over the rise, where she found herself at the dog town. Just then two great prairie hawks came skimming like pirates over the plain. As soon as they were in sight the prairie dogs all barked, jerking their tails at each bark, and hid below. When all were gone Tito walked on toward the hole of the big fat fellow whose body she coveted, and dropping the apple on the ground a couple of feet from the rim of the crater that formed his home, she put her nose down to enjoy the delicious smell of dog fat. Even his den smelled more fragrant than those of the rest. Then she went quietly behind a greasewood bush, in a lower place some twenty yards away, and lay flat. After a few seconds some venturesome prairie dog looked out, and seeing nothing, gave the 'all's well' bark. One by one they came out, and in twenty minutes the town was alive as before. One of the last to come out was the fat old Alderman. He always took good care of his own precious self. He peered out cautiously a few times, then climbed to the top of his lookout. A prairie dog hole is shaped like a funnel, going straight down. Around the top of this is built a high ridge which serves as a lookout, and also makes sure that, no matter how they may slip in their hurry, they are certain to drop into the funnel and be swallowed up by the all protecting earth. On the outside the ground slopes away gently from the funnel. Now, when the Alderman saw that strange round thing at his threshold he was afraid. Second inspection led him to believe that it was not dangerous, but was probably interesting. He went cautiously toward it, smelled it, and tried to nibble it; but the apple rolled away, for it was round, and the ground was smooth as well as sloping. The prairie dog followed and gave it a nip which satisfied him that the strange object would make good eating. But each time he nibbled, it rolled farther away. The coast seemed clear, all the other prairie dogs were out, so the fat Alderman did not hesitate to follow up the dodging, shifting apple.

The Alderman and the apple.

This way and that it wiggled, and he followed. Of course it worked toward the low place where grew the greasewood bush. The little tastes of apple that he got only whetted his appetite. The Alderman was more and more interested. Foot by foot he was led from his hole toward that old, familiar bush, and had no thought of anything but the joy of eating. And Tito curled herself and braced her sinewy legs, and measured the distance between, until it dwindled to not more than three good jumps; then up and like an arrow she went, and grabbed and bore him off at last.

Now it will never be known whether it was accident or design that led to the placing of that apple, but it proved important, and if such a thing were to happen once or twice to a smart coyote,—and it is usually clever ones that get such chances,—it might easily grow into a new trick of hunting.

After a hearty meal Tito buried the rest in a cold place, not to get rid of it, but to hide it for future use; and a little later, when she was too weak to hunt much, her various hoards of this sort came in very useful. True, the meat had turned very strong; but Tito was not critical, and she had no fears or theories of microbes, so suffered no ill effects.

VIII

The lovely Hiawathan spring was touching all things in the fairy Badlands. Oh, why are they called Badlands? If Nature sat down deliberately on the eighth day of creation and said, "Now work is done, let's play; let's make a place that shall combine everything that is finished and wonderful and beautiful—a paradise for man and bird and beast," it was surely then that she made these wild, fantastic hills, teeming with life, radiant with gayest flowers, varied with sylvan groves, bright with prairie sweeps and brimming lakes and streams. In foreground, offing, and distant hills that change at every step, we find some proof that Nature squandered here the riches that in other lands she used as sparingly as gold, with colorful sky above and colorful land below, and the distance blocked by sculptured buttes that are built of precious stones and ores, and tinged as by a lasting and unspeakable sunset. And yet, for all this ten times gorgeous wonderland enchanted, blind man had found no better name than one which says, the road to it is hard.

The little hollow west of Chimney Butte was freshly grassed. The dangerous looking Spanish bayonets, that through the bygone winter had waged war with all things, now sent out their contribution to the peaceful triumph of the spring, in flowers that have stirred even the chilly scientists to name them Gloriosa;

and the cactus, poisonous, most reptilian of herbs, surprised the world with a splendid bloom as little like itself as the pearl is like its mother shell fish. The sage and the greasewood lent their gold, and the sand anemone tinged the Badland hills like bluish snow; and in the air and earth and hills on every hand was felt the fecund promise of the spring. This was the end of the winter famine, the beginning of the summer feast, and this was the time the All-Mother ordained when first the little coyotes should see the light of day.

A mother does not have to learn to love her helpless, squirming brood. They bring the love with them—not much or little, not measurable, but perfect love. And in the dimly lighted warm abode she fondled them and licked them and cuddled them with heartful warmth of tenderness that was as much a new epoch in her life as in theirs.

But the pleasure of loving them was measured in the same measure as anxiety for their safety. In bygone days her care had been mainly for herself. All she had learned in her strange puppyhood, all she had picked up since, was bent to the main idea of self preservation. Now she was ousted from her own affections by her brood. Her chief care was to keep their home concealed, and this was not very hard at first, for she left them only when she must, to supply her own wants.

She came and went with great care, and only after spying well the land so that none should see and find the place of her treasure. If it were possible for the little ones' idea of their mother and the cowboys' idea to be set side by side they would be found to have nothing in common, though both were right in their point of view.

Tito and her brood.

The ranchmen knew the coyote only as a pair of despicable, cruel jaws, borne around on tireless legs, steered by incredible cunning, and leaving behind a track of destruction. The little ones knew her as a loving, gentle, all powerful guardian. For them her breast was soft and warm and infinitely tender. She fed and warmed them, she was their wise and watchful keeper. She was always at hand with food when they hungered, with wisdom to foil the cunning of their foes, and with a heart of courage tried to crown her well laid plans for them with uniform success.

A baby coyote is a shapeless, senseless, wriggling, and—to every one but its mother—a most uninteresting little lump. But after its eyes are open, after it has developed its legs, after it has learned to play in the sun with its brothers, or run at the gentle call of its mother when she brings home game for it to feed on, the baby coyote becomes one of the cutest, dearest little rascals on earth. And when the nine that made up Coyotito's brood had reached this stage, it did not require the glamour of motherhood to make them objects of the greatest interest.

The summer was now on. The little ones were beginning to eat flesh meat, and Tito, with some assistance from Saddleback, was kept busy to supply both themselves and the brood. Sometimes she brought them a prairie dog, at other times she would come home with a whole bunch of gophers and mice in her jaws; and once or twice, by the clever trick of relay chasing, she succeeded in getting one of the big northern jackrabbits for the little folks at home.

After they had feasted they would lie around in the sun for a time. Tito would mount guard on a bank and scan the earth and air with her keen, brassy eye, lest any dangerous foe would find their happy valley; and the merry pups played little games of tag, or chased the butterflies, or had apparently desperate encounters with each other, or tore and worried the bones and feathers that now lay about the threshold of the home. One, the least, for there is usually a runt, stayed near the mother and climbed on her back or pulled at her tail. They made a lovely picture as they played, and the wrestling group in the middle seemed the  focus of it all at first; but a keener, later look would have rested on the mother, quiet, watchful, not without anxiety, but, above all, with a face full of motherly tenderness. Oh, she was so proud and happy, and she would sit there and watch them and silently love them till it was time to go home, or until some sign of distant danger showed. Then, with a low growl, she gave the signal, and all disappeared from sight in a twinkling, after which she would set off to meet and turn the danger, or go on a fresh hunt for food.

IX

Wolver Jake have several plans for making a fortune, but each in turn was abandoned as soon as he found that it meant work. At one time or other most men of this kind see the chance of their lives in a poultry farm. They cherish the idea that somehow the poultry do all the work. And without troubling himself about the details, Jake devoted an unexpected windfall to the purchase of a dozen turkeys for his latest scheme. The turkeys were duly housed in one end of Jake's shanty, so as to be well guarded, and for a couple of days were the object of absorbing interest, and had the best of care—too much, really. But Jake's ardor waned about the third day; then the recurrent necessity of long celebrations at Medora, and the ancient allurements of idle hours spent lying on the tops of sunny buttes and of days spent sponging on the hospitality of distant ranches, swept away the last pretense of attention to his poultry farm. The turkeys were utterly neglected—left to forage for themselves; and each time that Jake returned to his uninviting shanty, after a few days' absence, he found fewer birds, till at last none but the old gobbler was left.

Jake cared little about the loss, but was filled with indignation against the thief.

He was now installed as wolver to the Broad Arrow outfit. That is, he was supplied with poison, traps, and horses and was also entitled to all he could make out of wolf bounties. A reliable man would have gotten pay in addition, for the ranchmen are generous, but Jake was not reliable. Every wolver knows, of course, that his business drops into several well marked periods.

In the later winter and early spring—the love season—the hounds will not hunt a she wolf. They will quit the trail of a he wolf at this time to take up that of a she wolf, but when they do overtake her, they, for some sentimental reason, invariably let her go in peace. In August and September the young coyotes and wolves are just beginning to run alone, and they are then easily trapped and poisoned. A month or so later the survivors have learned how to take care of themselves, but in the early summer the wolver knows that there are dens full of little ones all through the hills. Each den has from five to fifteen pups, and the only difficulty is to know the whereabouts of these family homes.

One way of finding the dens is to watch from some tall butte for a coyote carrying food to its brood. As this kind of wolving involved much lying still, it suited Jake very well. So, equipped with a Broad Arrow horse and the boss's field glasses, he put in week after week at den hunting—that is, lying asleep in some possible lookout, with an occasional glance over the country when it seemed easier to do that than to lie still.

The coyotes had learned to avoid the open. They generally went homeward along the sheltered hollows; but this was not always possible, and one day, while exercising his arduous profession in the country west of Chimney Butte, Jake's glasses and glance fell by chance on a dark spot which moved along an open hillside. It was grey , and even Jake knew that it was a coyote.

He made careful note of the place, and returned there next day to watch, selecting a high butte near where he had seen the coyote carrying the food. But all day passed, and he saw nothing. Next day, however, he descried a dark coyote, old Saddleback, carrying a large bird, and by the help of the glasses he made out that it was a turkey, and then he knew that the yard at home was quite empty, and he also knew where the rest of them had gone, and vowed terrible vengeance when he should find the den. He followed Saddleback with his eyes as far as possible, and that was no great way, then went to the place to see if he could track him any farther; but he found no guiding signs, and he did not chance on the little hollow that was the playground of Tito's brood.

Meanwhile Saddleback came to the little hollow and gave the low call that always conjured from the earth the unruly procession of the nine riotous little pups, and they dashed at the turkey and pulled and worried till it was torn up, and each that got a piece ran to one side alone and silently proceeded to eat, seizing his portion in his jaws when another came near, and growling his tiny growl as he showed the brownish whites of his eyes in his effort to watch the intruder. Those that got the softer parts to feed on were well fed. But the three that did not turned all their energies on the frame of the gobbler, and over that there waged a battle royal. This way and that they tugged and tussled, getting off occasional scraps, but really hindering each other feeding, till Tito glided in and deftly cut the turkey into three or four, when each dashed off with a prize, over which he sat and chewed and smacked his lips and jammed his head down sideways to bring the backmost teeth to bear, while the baby runt scrambled into the home den, carrying in triumph his share—the gobbler's grotesque head and neck.

X

Jake felt that he had been grievously wronged, indeed ruined, by that coyote that stole his turkeys. He vowed he would skin them alive when he found the pups, and took pleasure in thinking about how he would do it. His attempt to follow Saddleback by trailing was a failure, and all his searching for the den was useless, but he had come prepared for any emergency. In case he found the den he had brought a pick and shovel; in case he did not he had brought a living white hen.

The hen he now took to a broad open place near where he had seen Saddleback, and there he tethered her to a stick of wood that she could barely drag. Then he made himself comfortable on a lookout that was near, and lay still to watch. The hen, of course, ran to the end of the string, and then lay on the ground flopping stupidly. Presently the clog gave enough to ease the strain, she turned by mere chance in another direction, and so, for a time, stood up to look around.

The day went slowly by, and Jake lazily stretched himself on the blanket in his spying place. Toward evening Tito came by on a hunt. This was not surprising, for the den was only half a mile away. Tito had learned, among other rules, this, "Never show yourself on the sky line." In former days the coyotes used to trot along the tops of the ridges for the sake of the chance to watch both sides. But men and guns had taught Tito that in this way you are sure to be seen. She therefore made a practice of running along near the top, and once in a while peeping over.

This was what she did that evening as she went out to hunt for the children's supper, and her keen eyes fell on the white hen, stupidly stalking about and turning up its eyes in a wise way each time a harmless turkey buzzard came in sight against a huge white cloud.

Tito was puzzled. This was something new. It looked like game, but she feared to take any chances. She circled all around without showing herself, then decided that, whatever it might be, it was better let alone. As she passed on, a faint whiff of smoke caught her attention. She followed cautiously, and under a butte far from the hen she found Jake's camp. His bed was there, his horse was picketed, and on the remains of the fire was a pot which gave out a smell which she well knew about men's camps—the smell of coffee. Tito felt uneasy at this proof that a man was staying so near her home, but she went off quietly on her hunt, keeping out of sight, and Jake knew nothing of her visit.

About sundown he took in his decoy hen, as owls were abundant, and went back to his camp.

XI

Next day the hen was again put out, and late that afternoon Saddleback came trotting by. As soon as his eye fell on the white hen he stopped short, his head on one side, and gazed. Then he circled to get the wind, and went cautiously sneaking nearer, very cautiously, somewhat puzzled, till he got a whiff that reminded him of the place where he had found those turkeys. The hen took alarm, and tried to run away; but Saddleback made a rush, seized the hen so fiercely that the string was broken, and away he dashed toward the home valley.

Jake had fallen asleep, but the squawk of the hen happened to awaken him, and he sat up in time to see her borne away in old Saddleback's jaws.

As soon as they were out of sight Jake took up the white feather trail. At first it was easily followed, for the hen had shed plenty of plumes in her struggles; but once she was dead in Saddleback's jaws, very few feathers were dropped except where she was carried through the brush. But Jake was following quietly and certainly, for Saddleback had gone nearly in a straight line home to the little ones with the dangerous telltale prize. Once or twice there was a puzzling delay when the coyote had changed his course or gone over an open place; but one white feather was good for fifty yards, and when the daylight was gone, Jake was not two hundred yards from the hollow, in which at that very moment were the nine little pups, having a perfectly delightful time with the hen, pulling it to pieces, feasting and growling, sneezing the white feathers from their noses or coughing them from their throats.

If a puff of wind had now blown from them toward Jake, it might have carried a flurry of snowy plumes or even the merry cries of the revellers, and the den would have been discovered at once. But, as luck would have it, the evening lull was on, and all distant sounds were hidden by the crashing that Jake made in trying to trace his feather guides through the last thicket.

About this time Tito was returning home with a magpie that she had captured by watching till it went to feed within the ribs of a dead horse, when she ran across

Jake's trail. Now, a man on foot is always a suspicious character in this country. She followed the trail for a little to see where he was going, and that she knew at once from the scent. How it tells her no one can say, yet all hunters know that it does. And Tito marked that it was going straight toward her home. Thrilled with new fear, she hid the bird she was carrying, then followed the trail of the man. Within a few minutes she could hear him in the thicket, and Tito realized the terrible danger that was threatening. She went swiftly, quietly around to the den hollow, came on the heedless little roisterers, after giving the signal call, which prevented them taking alarm at her approach; but she must have had a shock when she saw how marked the hollow and the den were now, all drifted over with feathers white as snow. Then she gave the danger call that sent them all to earth, and the little glade was still.

Her own nose was so thoroughly and always her guide that it was not likely she thought of the white feathers being the telltale. But now she realized that a man, one she knew of old as a treacherous character, one whose scent had always meant mischief to her, that had been associated with all her own troubles and the cause of nearly all her desperate danger, was close to her darlings; was tracking them down; in a few minutes would surely have them in his merciless power.

Oh, the wrench to the mother's heart at the thought of what she could foresee! But the warmth of the mother-love lent life to the mother-wit. Having sent the little ones out of sight, and by a sign conveyed to Saddleback her alarm, she swiftly came back to the man, then she crossed before him, thinking, in her half-reasoning way, that the man must be following a foot-scent just as she herself would do, but would, of course, take the stronger line of tracks she was now laying. She did not realize that the failing daylight made any difference. Then she trotted to one side, and to make doubly sure of being followed, she uttered the fiercest challenges she could, just as many a time she had done to make the dogs pursue her,

Grrr-wow-wow-w-a-a-a-h,

and stood still; then ran a little nearer and did it again, and then again much nearer, and repeated her bark, she was so determined that the wolver should follow her.

Of course the wolver could see nothing of the coyote, for the shades were falling. He had to give up the hunt anyway. His understanding of the details was as different as possible from that the mother coyote had, and yet it came to the same thing. He recognized that the coyote's bark was the voice of the distressed mother trying to call him away. So he knew the brood must be close at hand, and all he now had to do was return in the morning and complete his search. So he made his way back to his camp.

XII

Saddleback thought they had won the victory. He felt secure, because the foot scent that he might have supposed the man to be following would be stale by morning. Tito did not feel so safe. That two legged beast was close to her home and her little ones; had barely been turned aside; might come back yet.

The wolver watered and repicketed his horse, kindled the fire anew, made his coffee and ate his evening meal, then smoked awhile before lying down to sleep, thinking occasionally of the little woolly scalps he expected to gather in the morning.

He was about to roll up in his blanket when, out of the dark distance, there sounded the evening cry of the coyote, the rolling challenge of more than one voice. Jake grinned in fiendish glee, and said, "There you are all right. Howl some more. I'll see you in the morning."

It was the ordinary, or rather one of the ordinary, camp calls of the coyote. It was sounded once, and then all was still. Jake soon forgot it in his loggish slumber.

The callers were Tito and Saddleback. The challenge was not an empty bluff. It had a distinct purpose behind it—to know for sure whether the enemy had any dogs with him; and because there was no responsive bark Tito knew that he had none.

Then Tito waited for an hour or so till the flickering fire had gone dead, and the only sound of life about the camp was the cropping of the grass by the picketed horse. Tito crept near softly, so softly that the horse did not see her till she was within twenty feet; then he gave a start that swung the tightened picket rope up into the air, and snorted gently. Tito went quietly forward, and opening her wide gape, took the rope in, almost under her ears, between the great scissor-like back teeth, then chewed it for a few seconds. The fibers quickly frayed, and, aided by the strain the nervous horse still kept up, the last of the strands gave way, and the horse

was free. He was not much alarmed; he knew the smell of coyote; and after jumping three steps and walking six, he stopped.

The sounding thumps of his hoofs on the ground awoke the sleeper. He looked up, but, seeing the horse standing there, he went calmly off to sleep again, supposing that all went well.

Tito had sneaked away, but she now returned like a shadow, avoided the sleeper, but came around, sniffed doubtfully at the coffee, and then puzzled over a tin can, while Saddleback, examined the frying pan full of "camp sinkers" and then defiled both cakes and pan with dirt. The bridle hung on a low bush; the coyotes did not know what it was, but just for luck they cut it into several pieces, then, taking the sacks that held Jake's bacon and flour, they carried them far away and buried them in the sand.

Having done all the mischief she could, Tito followed by her mate, now set off for a wooded gully some miles away, where was a hole that had been made first by a chipmunk, but enlarged by several other animals, including a fox that had tried to dig out its occupants. Tito stopped and looked at many possible places before she settled on this. Then she set to work to dig. Saddleback had followed in a half- comprehending way, till he saw what she was doing. Then when she, tired with digging, came out, he went into the hole, and after snuffing about went on with the work, throwing out the earth between his hind legs; and when it was piled up behind he would come out and push it yet farther away.

And so they worked for hours, not a word said, and yet with a sufficient comprehension of the object in view to work in relief of each other. And by the time the morning came they had a den big enough to do for their home, in case they must move, though it would not compare with the one in the grassy hollow.

XIII

It was nearly sunrise before the wolver awoke. With the true instinct of a plainsman he turned to look for the horse. It was gone. What his ship is to the sailor, what wings are to the bird, what money is to the merchant, the horse is to the plainsman. Without it he is helpless, lost at sea, wing broken, crippled in business. Afoot on the plains is the sum of earthly terrors. Even Jake realized this, and ere his foggy wits had fully felt the shock he sighted the steed afar on a flat, grazing and stepping ever farther from the camp. At a second glance Jake noticed that the horse was trailing the rope. If the rope had been left behind Jake would have known that it was hopeless to try to catch him; he would have finished his den hunt and found the little coyotes. But, with the trailing rope, there was a good chance of catching the horse; so Jake set out to try.

Of all maddening things there is nothing worse than to be almost, but not quite, able to catch your horse. Do what he might, Jake could not get quite near enough to seize the short rope, and the horse led him on and on, until at last they were well on the homeward trail.

Now Jake was afoot anyhow, so seeing no better plan, he set out to follow that horse right back to the ranch.

But when about seven miles were covered Jake succeeded in catching him. He rigged up a rough hackamore with the rope and rode bareback in fifteen minutes over the three miles that lay between him and sheep ranch, giving vent all the way to his pent up feelings in cruel abuse of that horse. Of course it did not do any good, and he knew that, but he considered it was heaps of satisfaction.

Here Jake got a meal and borrowed a saddle and a mongrel hound that could run a trail, and returned late in the afternoon to finish his den hunt. Had he known it, he now could have found it without the aid of the cur, for it was really close at hand when he took up the feather trail where last he had left it. Within one hundred yards he rose to the top of the little ridge; then just over it, almost face to face he came on a coyote, carrying in its mouth a large rabbit. The coyote leaped just at the same moment that Jake fired his revolver, and the dog broke into a fierce yelling and dashed off in pursuit, while Jake blazed and blazed away, without effect, and wondered why the coyote should still hang on to the rabbit as she ran for her life with the dog yelling at her heels. Jake followed as far as he could and fired at each chance, but scored no hit. So when they had vanished among the buttes he left the dog to follow or come back as he pleased, while he returned to the den, which, of course, was plain enough now. Jake knew that the pups were there yet. Had he not seen the mother bringing a rabbit for them?

So he set to work with pick and shovel all the rest of that day. There were plenty of signs that the den had inhabitants, and, duly encouraged, he dug on, and after several hours of the hardest work he have ever done, he came to the end of the den, only to find it empty. After cursing his luck at the first shock of disgust, he put on his strong leather glove and groped about in the nest. He felt something firm and drew it out. It was the head and neck of his own turkey gobbler, and that was all he got for his pains.

XIV

Tito had not been idle during the time that the enemy was horse hunting. Whatever Saddleback might have done, Tito would live in no fool's paradise. Having finished the new den, she trotted back to the little valley of feathers, and the first young one that came to meet her at the door of this home was a broad headed one much like herself. She seized him by the neck and set off, carrying him across country toward the new den, a couple of miles away. Every little while she had to put her offspring down to rest and give it chance to breathe. This made the moving slow, and the labor of transporting the pups occupied all that day, for Saddleback was not allowed to carry any of them, probably because he was too rough.

Beginning with the biggest and brightest, they were carried away one at a time, and late in the afternoon only the runt was left. Tito had not only worked at digging all night, she had also trotted over thirty miles, half of it with a heavy baby to carry. But she did not rest. She was just coming out of the den, carrying her youngest in her mouth, when over the very edge of this hollow appeared the mongrel hound, and a little way behind him Wolver Jake.

Away went Tito, holding the baby tight, and away went the dog behind her.

Bang! Bang! Bang! said the revolver.

But not a shot touched her. Then over the ridge they dashed, where the revolver could not reach her, and sped across a flat, the tired coyote and her baby, and the big fierce hound behind her, bounding his hardest. Had she been fresh and unweighted she could soon have left the clumsy cur that now was barking furiously on her track and rather gaining than losing in the race. But she put forth all her strength, careered along a slope, where she gained a little, then down across a brushy flat where the cruel bushes robbed her of all she had gained. But again into the open they came, and the wolver, laboring far behind, got sight of them and fired again and again with his revolver, and only stirred the dust, but still it made her dodge and lose time, and it also spurred the

Tito's race for life.

dog. The hunter saw the coyote, his old acquaintance of the bobtail, carrying still, as he thought, the jack rabbit she had been bringing to her brood, and wondered at her strange persistence. "Why doesn't she drop that weight when flying for her life?" But on she went and gamely bore her load over the hills, the man cursing his luck that he had not brought his horse, and the mongrel bounding in deadly earnest but thirty feet behind her. Then suddenly in front of Tito yawned a little cut bank gully. Tired and weighted, she dare not try the leap; she skirted around. But the dog was fresh; he cleared it easily, and the mother's start was cut down by half. But on she went, straining to hold the little one high above the scratching brush and the dangerous bayonet spikes; but straining too much, for the helpless cub was choking in his mother's grip. She must lay him down or strangle him; with such a weight she could not much longer keep out of reach. She tried to give the howl for help, but her voice was muffled by the cub, now struggling for breath, and as she tried to ease her grip on him a sudden wrench jerked him from her mouth into the grass—into the power of the merciless hound. Tito was far smaller than the dog; ordinarily she would have held him in fear; but her little one, her baby, was the only thought now, and as the brute sprang forward to tear it in his wicked jaws, she leaped between and stood facing him with all her mane erect, her teeth exposed, and plainly showed her resolve to save her young one at any price. The dog was not brave, only confident that he was bigger and had the man behind him. But the man was far away, and balked in his first rush at the trembling little coyote, that tried to hide in the grass, the cur hesitated a moment, and Tito howled the howl for help—the muster call:

Yap-yap-yap-yah-yah-yah-h-h-h-h,

and made the buttes around echo so that Jake could not tell where it came from; but some one else there was that heard and did know whence it came. The dog's courage revived on hearing something like a far away shout. Again he sprang at the little one, but again the mother balked him with her own body, and then they closed in deadly struggle. "Oh, if Saddleback would only come!" But no one came, and now she had no further chance to call. Weight is everything in a closing fight, and Tito soon went down, bravely fighting to the last, but clearly worsted; and the hound's courage grew with the sight of victory, and all he thought of now was to finish her and then kill her helpless baby in its turn. He had no ears or eyes for any other thing, till out of the nearest sage there flashed a streak of grey, and in a trice the big-voiced coward was hurled back by a foe almost as heavy as himself—hurled back with a crippled shoulder. Dash, chop, and stanch old Saddleback sprang on him again. Tito struggled to her feet, and they closed on him together. His courage fled at once when he saw the odds, and all he wanted now was safe escape—escape from Saddleback, whose speed was like the wind, escape from Tito, whose baby's life was at stake. Not twenty jumps away did he get; not breath enough had he to howl for help to his master in the distant hills; not fifteen yards away from her little one that he meant to tear, they tore him all to bits.

And Tito lifted the rescued young one, and traveling as slowly as she wished, they reached the new made den. There the family safely reunited, far away from danger of further attack by Wolver Jake or his kind.

And there they lived in peace till their mother had finished their training, and every one of them grew up wise in the ancient learning of the plains, wise in the later wisdom that the ranchers' war has forced upon them, and not only they, but their children's children, too.

The buffalo herds have gone; they have succumbed to the rifles of the hunters. The antelope droves are nearly gone; hound and lead were too much for them. The blacktail bands have dwindled before axe and fence. The ancient dwellers of the Badlands have faded like snow under the new conditions, but the coyotes are no more in fear of extinction. Their morning and evening song still sounds from the level buttes, as it did long years ago when every plain was a teeming land of game. They have learned the deadly secrets of traps and poisons, they know how to baffle the gunner and hound, they have matched their wits with the hunter's wits. They have learned how to prosper in a land of man-made plenty, in spite of the worst that man can do, and it was Tito that taught them how.

Badlands Billy
The Wolf that Won

While visiting Howard Eaton's Custer Trail Ranch in the Dakota Badlands in September of 1897, Seton learned about a marauding wolf named Mountain Billy. The wolf had been killing cattle on Badlands ranches since 1894, and his notoriety among the ranchers equaled that of Lobo in New Mexico. He, like Lobo, was also too intelligent to be caught in traps or to eat poisoned meat.

Seton rode with Eaton and several others during his stay in the Badlands in an attempt to run down Billy. They took along dogs to trail the wolf once his scent had been found. For three days the hunters unsuccessfully searched for the wolf in temperatures that reached one hundred degrees. Mountain Billy easily eluded the weary party, and Seton simply recorded in his journal, "wolf hunt unsuccessful."

Nevertheless, Seton learned enough about Billy that he was inspired to tell this story that appeared in his book, *Animal Heroes*, in 1905.

Badlands Billy
The Wolf that Won

I
The Howl by Night

Do you know the three calls of the hunting wolf; the long-drawn deep howl, the muster, that tells of game discovered but too strong for the finder to manage alone; and the higher ululation that ringing and swelling is the cry of the pack on a hot scent; and the sharp bark coupled with a short howl that, seeming least of all, is yet a gong of doom, for this is the cry "Close in, this is the finish."

We were riding the Badlands Buttes, King and I, with a pack of various hunting dogs stringing behind or trotting alongside. The sun had gone from the sky, and a blood-streak marked the spot where he died, away over Sentinel Butte. The hills were dim, the valleys dark, when from the nearest gloom there rolled a long-drawn cry that all men recognize instinctively—melodious, yet with a tone in it that sends a shudder up the spine, though now it has lost all menace for mankind. We listened for a moment. It was the wolf-hunter who broke silence, "That's Badlands Billy, ain't it a voice? He's out for his beef tonight."

II
Ancient Days

In pristine days the buffalo herds were followed by bands of wolves that preyed on the sick, the weak, and the wounded. When the buffalo were exterminated

the wolves were hard put for support, but the cattle came and solved the question for them by taking the buffalo's place. This caused the wolf war. The ranchmen offered a bounty for each wolf killed, and every cowboy out of work, was supplied with traps and poison for wolf killing. The very expert made this their sole business and became known as wolvers. King Ryder was one of these. He was a quiet, gentle-spoken fellow, with a keen eye and an insight into animal life that gave him special power over broncos and dogs, as well as wolves and bears, though in the last two cases it was power merely to surmise where they were and how best to get at them. He had been a wolver for years, and greatly surprised me by saying that "never in all his experience had he known a grey wolf to attack a human being."

We had many camp fire talks while the other men were sleeping, and then it was I learned the little that he knew about Badlands Billy. "Six times have I seen him and the seventh will be Sunday, you bet. He takes his long rest then." And thus on the very ground where it all fell out, to the noise of the night wind and the yapping of the coyote, interrupted sometimes by the deep-drawn howl of the hero himself, I heard chapters of this history which, with others gleaned in many fields, gave me the story of the Big Dark Wolf of Sentinel Butte.

III
In the Canyon

Away back in the spring of 1892 a wolver was working on the east side of the Sentinel Mountain that so long was a principal landmark of the old plainsmen. Pelts were not good in May, but the bounties were high, five dollars a head, and double for she wolves. As he went down to the creek one morning he saw a wolf coming to drink on the other side. He had an easy shot, and on killing it found it was a nursing she

wolf. Evidently her family was somewhere near, so he spent two or three day searching in all the likely places, but found no clue to the den.

Two weeks afterward, as the wolver rode down an adjoining canyon, he saw a wolf come out of a hole. The ever ready rifle flew up, and another ten dollar scalp was added to his string. Now he dug into the den and found the litter, a most surprising one indeed, for it consisted not of the usual five or six wolf pups, but of eleven, and these, strange to say, were of two sizes, five of them larger and older than the other six. Here were two distinct families with one mother, and as he added their scalps to his string of trophies the truth dawned on the hunter. One lot was surely the family of the she wolf he had killed two weeks before. The case was clear; the little ones awaiting the mother that was never to come, had whined piteously and more loudly as their hunger pangs increased; the other mother passing had heard the cubs; her heart was tender now, her own little ones had so recently come, and she cared for the orphans, carried them to her own den, and was providing for the double family when the rifleman had cut the gentle chapter short.

Many a wolver has dug into a wolf den to find nothing. The old wolves or possibly the cubs themselves often dig little side pockets and off galleries, and when an enemy is breaking in they hide in these. The loose earth conceals the small pocket and thus the cubs escape. When the wolver retired with his scalps he did not know that the biggest of all the cubs, was still in the den, and even had he waited about for two hours, he might have been no wiser. Three hours later the sun went down and there was a slight scratching afar in the hole; first two little gray paws, then a small black nose appeared in a soft sand pile to one side of the den. At length the cub came forth from his hiding. He had been frightened by the attack on the den; now he was perplexed by its condition.

It was thrice as large as it had been and open at the top now. Lying near were things that smelled like his brothers and sisters, but they were repellent to him. He was filled with fear as he sniffed at them, and sneaked aside into a thicket of grass, as a night hawk boomed over his head. He crouched all night in that thicket. He did not dare to go near the den, and knew not where else he could go. The next morning when two vultures came swooping down on the bodies, the wolf cub ran off in the thicket, and seeing its deepest cover, was led down a ravine to a wide valley. Suddenly there arose from the grass a big she wolf, like his mother, yet different, a stranger, and instinctively the stray cub sank to the earth, as the old wolf bounded on him. No doubt the cub had been taken for some lawful prey, but a whiff set that right. She stood over him for an instant. He groveled at her feet. The impulse to kill him or at least give him a shake died away. He had the smell of a young cub. Her own were about his age, her heart was touched, and when he found courage enough to put his nose up and smell her nose, she made no angry demonstration except a short half-hearted growl. Now, however, he had smelled something that he sorely needed. He had not fed since the day before, and when the old wolf turned to leave him, he tumbled after her on clumsy puppy legs. Had the mother wolf been far from home he must soon have been left behind, but the nearest hollow was the chosen place, and the cub arrived at the den's mouth soon after the mother wolf.

A stranger is an enemy, and the old one rushing forth to the defense, met the cub again, and again was restrained by something that rose in her response to the smell. The cub had thrown himself on his back in utter submission, but that did not prevent his nose reporting to him the good thing almost within reach. The she wolf went into the den and curled herself about her brood; the cub persisted in following. She snarled as he approached her own little ones, but disarming wrath each time by submission and his very cubhood, he was presently among her brood, helping himself to what he wanted so greatly, and thus he adopted himself into her family. In a few days he was so much one of them that the mother forgot about his being a stranger. Yet he was different from them in several ways—older by two weeks, stronger, and marked on the neck and shoulders with what afterward grew to be a dark mane.

Little Duskymane could not have been happier in his choice of a foster mother, for the Yellow Wolf was not only a good hunter with a fund of cunning, but she was a wolf of modern ideas as well. The old tricks of tolling a prairie dog, relaying for antelope, houghing a bronco or flanking a steer she had learned partly from instinct and partly from the example of her more experienced relatives, when they joined to form the winter bands. But, just as necessary nowadays, she had learned that all men carry guns, that guns are irresistible, that the only way to avoid them is by keeping out of sight while the sun is up, and yet that at night they are harmless. She had a fair comprehension of traps, indeed she had been in one once, and though she left a toe behind in pulling free, it was a toe most advantageously disposed of; thenceforth, though not comprehending the nature of the trap, she was thoroughly imbued with the

Billy finds a foster mother.

horror of it, with the idea indeed that iron is dangerous, and at any price it should be avoided.

On one occasion, when she and five others were planning ro raid a sheep yard, she held back at the last minute because some new strung wires appeared. The others rushed in to find the sheep beyond their reach, themselves in a death trap.

Thus she had learned the newer dangers, and while it is unlikely that she had any clear mental conception of them she had acquired a wholesome distrust of all things strange, and a horror of one or two in particular that proved her lasting safeguard. Each year she raised her brood successfully and the number of yellow wolves increased in the country. Guns, traps, men and the new animals they brought had been learned, but there was yet another lesson before her—a terrible one indeed.

About the time Duskymane's brothers were a month old his foster mother returned in a strange condition. She was frothing at the mouth, her legs trembled, and she fell in a convulsion near the doorway of the den, but recovering, she came in. Her jaws quivered, her teeth rattled a little as she tried to lick the little ones; she seized her own front leg and bit it so as not to bite them, but at length she grew quieter and calmer. The cubs had retreated in fear to a far pocket, but now they returned and crowded about her to seek their usual food. The mother recovered, but was very ill for two or three days, and those days with the poison in her system worked disaster for the brood. They were terribly sick; only the strongest could survive, and when the trial of strength was over, the den contained only the old one and the black-maned cub, the one she had adopted. Thus little Duskymane became her sole charge; all her strength was devoted to feeding him, and he thrived apace.

Wolves are quick to learn certain things. The reactions of smell are the greatest that a wolf can feel, and thenceforth both cub and foster mother experienced a quick, unreasoning sense of fear and hate the moment the smell of strychnine reached them.

IV
The Rudiments of Wolf Training

With the sustenance of seven at his service the little wolf had every reason to grow, and when in the autumn he began to follow his mother on her hunting trips he was as tall as she was. Now a change of region was forced on them, for numbers of little wolves were growing up. Sentinel Butte, the rocky fastness of the plains, was claimed by many that were big and strong; the weaker must move out, and with them Yellow Wolf and the Dusky Cub.

Wolves have no language in the sense that man has; their vocabulary is probably limited to a dozen howls, barks, and grunts expressing the simplest emotions; but they have several other modes of conveying ideas, and one very special method of spreading information - the wolf telephone. Scattered over their range are a number of recognized "centrals." Sometimes these are stones, sometimes the angle of cross trails, sometimes a buffalo skull, indeed, any conspicuous object near a main trail is used. A wolf calling here, as a dog does at a telegraph post, or a muskrat at a certain mud pie point, leaves his body scent and learns what other visitors have been there recently to do the same. He learns also whence they came and where they went, as well as something about their condition, whether hunted, hungry, gorged, or sick. By this system of registration a wolf knows where his friends, as well as his foes, are to be found. And Duskymane, following after the Yellow Wolf, was taught the places and uses of the many signal stations without any conscious attempt at teaching on the part of his foster mother. Example backed by his native instincts was indeed the chief teacher, but on one occasion at least there was something very like the effort of a human parent to guard her child in danger.

The Dark Cub had learned the rudiments of wolf life; that the way to fight dogs is to run, and to fight as you run, never grapple, but snap, snap, snap, and make for the rough country where horses cannot bring their riders.

He learned not to bother about the coyotes that follow for the pickings when you hunt; you cannot catch them, and they do you no harm.

He knew he must not waste time dashing after birds that alight on the ground; and that he must keep away from the little black and white animal with the bushy tail. It is not very good to eat, and it is very, very bad to smell.

Poison! Oh, he never forgot that smell from the day when the den was cleared of all his foster brothers.

He now knew that the first move in attacking sheep was to scatter them; a lone sheep is a foolish and easy prey; that the way to round up a band of cattle was to frighten a calf.

He learned that he must always attack a steer behind, a sheep in front, and a horse in the middle, that is, on the flank, and never, never attack a man at all, never even face him. But an important lesson was added to these, one in which the mother consciously taught him of a secret foe.

V

The Lesson on Traps

A calf had died at branding time and now, two weeks later, was in its best state for perfect taste, not too fresh, not over ripe—that is, in a wolf's opinion—and the wind carried this information afar. The Yellow Wolf and Duskymane were out for supper, though not yet knowing where, when the tidings of veal arrived, and they trotted up the wind. The calf was in an open place, and plain to be seen in the moonlight. A dog would have trotted right up to the carcass, an old-time wolf might have done so, but constant war had developed constant vigilance in the Yellow Wolf, and trusting nothing and no one but her nose, she slacked her speed to a walk. On coming in easy view she stopped, and for long swung her nose, submitting the wind to the closest possible chemical analysis. She tried it with her finest tests, blew all the membranes clean again and tried it once more; and this was the report of the trusty nostrils, yes, the unanimous report. First, rich and racy smell of calf, seventy percent; smells of grass, bugs, wood, flowers, trees, sand, and other uninteresting negations, fifteen percent; smell of her cub and herself, positive but ignorable, ten percent; of sweaty leather smell, one percent; of human body scent, one-half percent; smell of iron, a trace.

The old wolf crouched a little but sniffed hard with swinging nose; the young wolf imitatively did the same. She backed off to a greater distance; the cub stood. She gave a low whine; he followed unwillingly. She circled around the tempting carcass; a new smell was recorded—coyotes trail scent, soon followed by coyote body scent. Yes, there they were sneaking along a near ridge, and now as she passed to one side the samples changed, the wind had lost nearly every trace of calf; miscellaneous, commonplace, and uninteresting smells were there instead. The human track scent was as before, the trace of leather was gone, but fully one-half percent of iron odor, and body smell of man raised to nearly two percent.

Fully alarmed, she conveyed her fear to the cub by her rigid pose, her air intent, and her slightly bristling mane.

She continued her round. At one time on a high place the human body scent was doubly strong, then as she dropped it faded. Then the wind brought the full calf odor with several track scents of coyotes and sundry birds. Her suspicions were lulling as in a smalling circle she neared the tempting feast from the windward side.

She had even advanced straight toward it for a few steps when the sweaty leather sang loud and strong again, and smoke and iron mingled like two strands of a part-colored yarn. Centering all her attention on this, she advanced within two leaps of the calf. There on the ground was a scrap of leather, telling also of a human touch, close at hand the calf, and now the iron and smoke on the full vast smell of calf were like a snake trail across the trail of a whole beef herd. It was so slight that the cub, with the appetite and impatience of youth, pressed up against his mother's shoulder to go past and eat without delay. She seized him by the neck and flung him back. A stone struck by his feet rolled forward and stopped with a peculiar clink. The danger smell was greatly increased at this, and the Yellow Wolf backed slowly from the feast, the cub unwillingly following.

As he looked wistfully he saw the coyotes drawing nearer, mindful chiefly to avoid the wolves. He watched their really cautious advance; it seemed like heedless rushing compared with his mother's approach. The calf smell rolled forth in exquisite and overpowering excellence now, for they were tearing the meat, when a sharp clank was heard and a yelp from a coyote. At the same time the quiet night was shocked with a roar and a flash of fire. Heavy shots spattered calf and coyotes, and yelping like beaten dogs they scattered, excepting one that was killed and a second struggling in the trap set here by the ever active wolvers. The air was charged with the hateful smells redoubled now, and horrid smells additional. The Yellow Wolf glided down a hollow and led her cub away in flight, but, as they went, they saw a man rush from the bank near where the mother's nose had warned her of the human scent. They saw him kill the caught coyote and set the traps for more.

Their narrow escape from trap and gun.

VI
The Beguiling of the Yellow Wolf

The life game is a hard game, for we may win ten thousand times, and if we fail but once our gain is gone. How many hundred times had the Yellow Wolf scorned the traps; how many cubs she had trained to do the same! Of all the dangers to her life she best knew traps.

October had come; the cub was now much taller than the mother. The wolver had seen them once—a yellow wolf followed by another, whose long, awkward legs, big, soft feet, thin neck, and skimpy tail proclaimed him this year's cub. The record of the dust and sand said that the old one had lost a right front toe, and that the young one was of giant size.

It was the wolver that thought to turn the carcass of the calf to profit, but he was disappointed in getting coyotes instead of wolves. It was the beginning of the trapping season, for this month fur is prime. A young trapper often fastens the bait on the trap; an experienced one does not. A good trapper will even put the bait at one place and the trap ten or twenty feet away, but at a spot that the wolf is likely to cross in circling. A favorite plan is to hide three or four traps around an open place, and scatter some scraps of meat in the middle. The traps are buried out of sight after being smoked to hide the taint of hands and iron. Sometimes no bait is used except a little piece of cotton or a tuft of feathers that may catch the wolf's eye or pique its curiosity and tempt it to circle on the fateful, treacherous ground. A good trapper varies his methods continually so that the wolves cannot learn his way. Their only safeguards are perpetual vigilance and distrust of all smells that are known to be of man.

The wolver, with a load of the strongest steel traps, had begun his autumn work on the Cottonwood.

An old buffalo trail crossing the river followed a little draw that climbed the hills to the level upland. All animals use these trails, wolves and foxes as well as cattle and deer; they are the main thoroughfares. A cottonwood stump not far from where it plunged to the gravelly stream was marked with wolf signs that told the wolver of its use. Here was an excellent place for traps, not on the trail, for cattle were here in numbers, but twenty yards away on a level, sandy spot he set four traps in a twelve foot square. Near each he scattered two or three scraps of meat; three or four white feathers on a spear of grass in the middle completed the setting. No human eye, few animal noses, could have detected the hidden danger of that sandy ground, when the sun and wind and the sand itself had dissipated the man track taint.

The Yellow Wolf had seen and passed, and taught her giant son to pass, such traps a thousand times before.

The cattle came to water in the heat of the day. They strung down the buffalo path as once the buffalo did. The little vesper birds flitted before them, the cow birds rode on them, and the prairie dogs chattered at them, just as they once did at the buffalo.

Down from the grey-green mesa with it green-grey rocks, they marched with imposing solemnity, importance, and directness of purpose. Some frolicsome calves playing alongside the trail, grew sober and walked behind their mothers as the river flat was reached. The old cow that headed the procession sniffed suspiciously as she passed the trap set, but it was far away, otherwise she would have pawed and bellowed over the scraps of bloody beef till every trap was sprung and harmless.

But she led to the river. After all had drunk their fill they lay down on the nearest bank till late afternoon. Then their unheard dinner gong aroused them, and started them on the backward march to where the richest pastures grew.

One or two small birds had picked at the scraps of meat, some blue-bottle flies buzzed about, but the sinking sun saw the sandy mask untouched.

A brown Marsh hawk came skimming over the river flat as the sun began his color play. Blackbirds dashed into thickets, and easily avoided his clumsy pounce. It was too early for the mice, but, as he skimmed the ground, his keen eye caught the flutter of feathers by the trap and turned his flight. The feathers in their uninteresting emptiness were exposed before he was near, but now he saw the scraps of meat. Guileless of cunning, he alighted and was devouring a second lump when—clank—the dust was flirted high and the Marsh hawk was held by his toes, struggling vainly in the jaws of a powerful wolf trap. He was not much hurt. His ample wings winnowed from time to time, in efforts to be free, but he was helpless, even as a sparrow might be in a rat trap, and when the sun had played his fierce chromatic scale, his swan song sung, and died as he dies only in the blazing west, and the shades had fallen on the melodramatic scene of the mouse in the elephant trap, there was a deep, rich sound on the high flat butte, answered by another, neither very long, neither repeated, and both instinctive rather than necessary. One was the muster call of an ordinary wolf, the other the answer of a very big male, not a pair in this case, but mother and son—Yellow Wolf and Duskymane. They came trotting together down the buffalo trail. They paused at the telephone box on the hill and again at the old cottonwood root, and were making for the river when the hawk in the trap fluttered his wings. The old wolf turned toward him, a wounded bird on the ground surely, and she rushed forward. Sun and sand soon burn all trail scents; there was nothing to warn her. She sprang on the flopping bird and a chop of her jaws ended his troubles, but a horrid sound—the gritting of her teeth on steel—told of her peril. She dropped the hawk and sprang backward from the dangerous ground, but landed in the second trap. High on her foot its death grip closed, and leaping with all her strength, to escape, she set her fore foot in another of the lurking grips of steel. Never had a trap been so baited before. Never was she so unsuspicious. Never was catch more sure. Fear and fury filled the old wolf's heart; she tugged and strained, she

.THE DESPAIR of THE YELLOW-WOLF

chewed the chains, she snarled and foamed. One trap with its buried log, she might have dragged; with two, she was helpless. Struggle as she might, it only worked those relentless jaws more deeply into her feet. She snapped wildly at the air; she tore the dead hawk into shreds; she roared the short, barking roar of a crazy wolf. She bit at the traps, at her cub, at herself. She tore her legs that were held; she gnawed in frenzy at her flank, she chopped off her tail in her madness; she splintered all her teeth on the steel, and filled her bleeding, foaming jaws with clay and sand.

She struggled til she fell, and writhed about or lay like dead, till strong enough to rise and grind the chains again with her teeth.

And so the night passed by.

And Duskymane? Where was he? The feeling of the time when his foster mother had come home poisoned, now returned; but he was even more afraid of her. She seemed filled with fighting hate. He held away and whined a little; he slunk off and came back when she lay still, only to retreat again, as she sprang forward, raging at him, and then renewed her efforts at the traps. He did not understand it, but he knew this much, she was in terrible trouble, and the cause seemed to be the same as that which had scared them the night they had ventured near the calf.

Duskymane hung about all night, fearing to go near, not knowing what to do, and helpless as his mother.

At dawn the next day a sheepherder seeking lost sheep discovered her from a neighboring hill. A signal mirror called the wolver from his camp. Duskymane saw the new danger. He was a mere cub, though so tall; he could not face the man and fled at his approach.

The wolver rode up to the sorry, tattered, bleeding she wolf in the trap. He raised his rifle and soon the struggling stopped.

The wolver read the trail and signs about, and remembering those he had read before, he divined that this was the wolf with the great cub - the she wolf of Sentinel Butte.

Duskymane heard the crack as he scurried off into cover. He could scarcely know what it meant, but he never saw his kind old foster mother again. Thenceforth he must face the world alone.

VII

The Young Wolf Wins a Place and Fame

Instinct is no doubt a wolf's first and best guide, but gifted parents are a great start in life. The dusky-maned cub had had a mother of rare excellence, and he reaped the advantage of all her cleverness. He had inherited an exquisite nose and had absolute confidence in it admonitions. Mankind has difficulty in recognizing the power of nostrils. A grey wolf can glance over the morning wind as a man does over his newspaper and get all the latest news. He can swing over the ground and have the minutest information of every living creature that has walked there within many hours. His nose even tells which way it ran, and in a word renders a statement of every animal that recently crossed his trail, whence it came, and whither it went.

That power had Duskymane in the highest degree; his broad, moist nose was evidence of it to all who are judges of such things. Added to this, his frame was of unusual power and endurance, and last, he had early learned a deep distrust of everything strange, and, call it what we will, shyness, wariness or suspicion, it was worth more to him than all his cleverness. It was this as much as his physical powers that made a success of his life. Might is right in wolf land, and Duskymane and his mother had been driven out of Sentinel Butte. But it was a very delectable land, and he kept drifting back to his native mountain. One or two big wolves there resented his coming. They drove him off several times, yet each time he returned he was better able to face them; and before he was eighteen months old he had defeated all rivals and established himself again on his native ground; where he lived like a robber baron, levying tribute on the rich lands about him and finding safety in the rocky fastness.

Wolver Ryder often hunted in that country, and before long, he came across a five and one-half inch track, the foot print of a giant wolf. Roughly reckoned, twenty to twenty-five pounds of weight or six inches of stature is a fair allowance for each inch of a wolf's foot; this wolf therefore stood thirty-three inches at the shoulder and weighed about one hundred and forty pounds, by far the largest wolf he had ever met. King had lived in goat country, and now in goat language he exclaimed, "You bet, ain't that an old billy?" Thus by trivial chance it was that Duskymane was known to his foe as Badlands Billy.

Ryder was familiar with the muster call of the wolves, the long, smooth cry, but Billy's had a singular feature, a slurring that was always distinctive. Ryder had heard this before, in the Cottonwood Canyon, and when at length he got a sight of the big wolf with the black mane, it struck him that this was also the cub of the old yellow fury that he had trapped.

These were among the things he told me as we sat by the fire at night. I knew of the early days when any one could trap or poison wolves, of the passing of those days, with the passing of the simple wolves; of the new race of wolves with new cunning that were defying the methods of the ranchmen, and increasing steadily in numbers. Now the wolver told me of the various ventures that Penroof had made with different kinds of hounds; of fox hounds too thin-skinned to fight; of greyhounds that were useless when the animal was out of sight; of Danes too heavy for the rough country, and, last, of the composite pack with some of all kinds, including at times a Bull terrier to lead them in the final fight.

He told of hunts after coyotes, which usually were successful because the coyotes sought the plains and were easily caught by the greyhounds. He told of killing some small grey wolves with this very pack, usually at the cost of the one that led them; but above all he dwelt on the wonderful prowess of "that thar cussed old black wolf of Sentinel Butte," and related the many attempts to run him down or corner him—an unbroken array of failures. For the big wolf, with exasperating persistence, continued to live on the finest stock of the Penroof brand, and each year was teaching more wolves how to do the same with perfect impunity.

I listened even as gold hunters listen to stories of treasure trove, for these were the things of my world. These things indeed were uppermost in all our minds, for the Penroof pack was lying around our camp fire now. We were out after Badlands Billy.

VIII
The Voice in the Night and the Big Track in the Morning

One night late in September after the last streak of light was gone from the west and the coyotes had begun their yapping chorus, a deep, booming sound was heard. King took out his pipe, turned his head and said, "That's him—that's old Billy. He's been watching us all day from some high place, and now when the guns are useless he's here to have a little fun with us."

Two or three dogs arose, with bristling manes, for they clearly recognized that this was no coyote. They rushed out into the night, but did not go far; their brawling sounds were suddenly varied by loud yelps, and they came running back to the shelter of the fire. One was so badly cut in the shoulder that he was useless for the rest of the hunt. Another was hurt in the flank— it seemed the less serious wound, and yet next morning the hunters buried that second dog.

The men were furious. They vowed speedy vengeance, and at dawn were off on the trail. The coyotes yelped their dawning song, but they melted into the hills when the light was strong. The hunters searched about for the big wolf's track, hoping that the hounds would

"'That's him.'"

be able to take it up and find him, but they either could not or would not.

They found a coyote, however, and within a few hundred yards they killed him. It was a victory, I suppose, for coyotes kill calves and sheep, but somehow I felt the common thought of all, "Mighty brave dogs for a little coyote, but they could not face the big wolf last night."

Young Penroof, as though in answer to one of the unput questions, said, "Say, boys, I believe old Billy had a hull bunch of wolves with him last night."

"Didn't see but one track," said King gruffly.

In this way the whole of October slipped by; all day hard riding after doubtful trails, following the dogs, who either could not keep the big trail or feared to do so, and again and again we had news of damage done by the wolf; sometimes a cowboy would report it to us, and sometimes we found the carcasses ourselves. A few of these we poisoned, though it is considered a very dangerous thing to do while running dogs. The end of the month found us a weather beaten, dispirited lot of men with a worn out lot of horses, and a foot-sore pack, reduced in numbers from ten to seven. So far we had killed only one grey wolf and three coyotes. Badlands Billy had killed at least a dozen cows and dogs at fifty dollars a head. Some of the boys decided to give it up and go home, so King took advantage of their going to send a letter asking for reenforcements including all the spare dogs at the ranch.

During the two days' wait we rested our horses, shot some game, and prepared for a harder hunt. Late on the second day the new dogs arrived—eight beauties—and raised the working pack to fifteen.

The weather now turned much cooler, and in the morning, to the joy of the wolvers, the ground was white with snow. This surely meant success. With cool weather for the dogs and horses to run; with the big wolf not far away, for he had been heard the night before; and with tracking snow, so that once found he could not baffle us, escape for him was impossible.

We were up at dawn, but before we could get away, three men came riding into camp. They were the Penroof boys back again. The change of weather had changed their minds; they knew that with snow we might have luck

"Remember now," said King, as all were mounting, "we don't want any but Badlands Billy this trip. Get him an' we kin bust up the hull combination. It is a five and a half inch track."

And each measured off on his quirt handle, or on his glove, the exact five and a half inches that was to be used in testing the tracks he might find.

Not more than an hour elapsed before we got a signal from the rider who had gone westward.

One shot that means "attention," a pause while counting ten, then two shots that means "come on."

King gathered the dogs and rode direct to the distant figure on the hill. All hearts beat high with hope, and we were not disappointed. Some small wolf tracks had been found, but here at last was the big track, nearly six inches long. Young Penroof wanted to yell and set out a full gallop. It was like hunting a lion; it was like finding happiness long deferred. The hunter knows nothing more inspiring than the clean cut line of fresh tracks that is leading to a wonderful animal he has long been hunting in vain. How King's eye gleamed as he gloated over the sign.

IX
Run Down at Last

It was the roughest of all rough riding. It was a far longer hunt than we had expected, and was full of little incidents, for that endless line of marks was minute history of all that the big wolf had done the night before. Here he had circled at the telephone box and looked for news; there he had paused to examine an old skull; here he had shied off and swung cautiously up wind to examine something that proved to be an old tin can; there at length he had mounted a low hill and sat down, probably giving the muster howl, for two wolves had come to him from different directions, and they then had descended to the river flat where the cattle would seek shelter during the storm. Here all three had visited a buffalo skull; there they trotted in line; and yonder they separated, going three different ways, to meet— yes—here—oh, what a sight, a fine cow ripped open, left dead and uneaten. Not to their taste, it seems, for see! within a mile is another killed by them. Not six hours ago, they had feasted.

Here their trails scatter again, but not far, and the snow tells plainly how each had lain down to sleep. The hounds' manes bristled as they sniffed those places. King had held the dogs well in hand, but now they were greatly excited. We came to a hill whereon the wolves had turned and faced our way, then fled at full speed,— so said the trail,—and now it was clear that they had watched us from that hill and were not far away.

The pack kept well together, because the greyhounds, seeing no quarry, were merely puttering about among the other dogs or running back with the horses. We went as fast as we could, for the wolves were speeding. Up mesas and down coulees we rode, sticking closely to the dogs, though it was the roughest country that could be picked. One gully after another, an hour and another hour, and still the three-fold track went bounding on; another hour and no change, but interminable climbing, sliding, struggling, through brush and over boulders, guided by the far away yelping of the dogs.

Now the chase led downward to the low valley of the river where there was scarcely any snow. Jumping and scrambling down hills, recklessly leaping dangerous gullies and slippery rocks, we felt that we could not hold out much longer; when on the lowest, driest level the pack split, some went up, some went down, and others straight on. Oh, how King did swear! He knew at once what it meant. The wolves had scattered and so had divided the pack, three dogs after a wolf would have no chance, four could not kill him, two would certainly be killed. And yet this was the first encouraging sign we had seen for it meant that the wolves were hard pressed.

We spurred ahead to stop the dogs, to pick for them the only trail. But that was not so easy. Without snow here and with countless dog tracks, we were foiled. All we could do was to let the dogs choose, but keep them to a single choice.

Away we went as before, hoping, yet fearing that we were not on the right track. The dogs ran well, very fast indeed. This was a bad sign, King said, but we could not get sight of the track because the dogs overran it before we came.

After a two mile run the chase led upward again in snow country; the wolf was sighted, but to our disgust, we were on the track of the smallest one.

"I thought so," growled young Penroof. "Dogs was altogether too keen for a serious proposition. Kind o' surprised it ain't turned out a Jack rabbit."

Within another mile he had turned to bay in a willow thicket. We heard him howl the long-drawn howl for help, and before we could reach the place King saw the dogs recoil and scatter. A minute later there sped from the far side of the thicket a small grey wolf and a black one of very much greater size.

"By golly, if he didn't yell for help, and Billy come back to help him, that's great!" exclaimed the wolver. And my heart went out to the brave old wolf that refused to escape by abandoning his friend.

The next hour was a hard repetition of the gully riding, but it was on the highlands where there was snow, and when again the pack was split, we strained every power and succeeded in keeping them on the big "five-fifty track" that already was wearing for me the glamour of romance.

Evidently the dogs preferred either of the others, but we got them going at last. Another half hour's hard work and far ahead, as I rose to a broad flat plain, I had my first glimpse of the Big Black Wolf of Sentinel Butte.

"Hurrah! Badlands Billy! Hurrah! Badlands Billy!" I shouted in salute, and the others took up the cry.

We were on his track at last, thanks to himself. The dogs joined in with a louder baying, the greyhounds yelped and made straight for him, and the horses sniffed and sprang more gamely as they caught the thrill. The only silent one was the black-maned wolf, and as I marked his size and power, and above all his long and massive jaws, I knew why the dogs preferred some other trail.

With head and tail low he was bounding over the snow. His tongue was lolling long; plainly he was hard pressed. The wolvers' hands flew to their revolvers, though he was three hundred yards ahead; they were

out for blood, not sport. But an instant later he had sunk from view in the nearest sheltered canyon.

Now which way would he go, up or down the canyon. Up was toward his mountain, down was better cover. King and I thought "up," so pressed westward along the ridge. But the others rode eastward, watching for a chance to shoot.

Soon we had ridden out of hearing. We were wrong, the wolf had gone down, but we heard no shooting. The canyon was crossable here; we reached the other side and then turned back at a gallop, scanning the snow for a trail, the hills for a moving form, or the wind for a sound of life.

"Squeak, squeak," went our saddle leathers, "puff, puff," our horses, and their feet, "ka-lump, ka-ka-lump."

X
When Billy went back to his Mountain

We were back opposite to where the wolf had plunged, but saw no sign. We rode at an easy gallop on eastward a mile and still on, when King gasped out, "Look at that!" A dark spot was moving on the snow ahead. We put on speed. Another dark spot appeared, and another, but they were not going fast. In five minutes we were near them, to find three of our own greyhounds. They had lost sight of the game and with that their interest waned. Now they were seeking us. We saw nothing there of the chase or of the other hunters. But hastening to the next ridge we stumbled on the trail we sought and followed as hard as though in view. Another canyon came in our path, and as we rode and looked for a place to cross, a wild din of hounds came from its brushy depth. The clamor grew and passed up the middle.

We raced along the rim, hoping to see the game. The dogs appeared near the farther side, not in a pack, but a long, straggling line. In five minutes more they rose to the edge, and ahead of them was the great black wolf. He was loping as before, head and tail low. Power was plain in every limb, and double power in his jaws and neck, but I thought his bounds were shorter now, and that they had lost their spring. The dogs slowly reached the upper level, and sighting him they broke into a feeble cry; they, too, were nearly spent. The greyhounds saw the chase, and leaving us they scrambled down the canyon and up the other side at impetuous speed that would surely break them down, while we rode, vainly seeking means of crossing.

How the wolver raved to see the pack lead off in the climax of the chase, and himself held up behind. But he rode and wrathed and still rode, up to where the canyon dwindled—rough land and a hard ride. As we neared the great flat mountain, the feeble cry of the pack was heard again from the south, then toward the high butte's side, and just a trifle louder now. We reined in on a hillock and scanned the snow. A moving speck appeared, then others, not bunched, but in a straggling train, and at times there was a far faint cry. They were headed toward us, coming on, yes! coming, but so slowly, for not one was really running now. There was the grim old cow killer limping over the ground, and far behind a greyhound, and another, and farther still, the other dogs in order of their speed, slowly, gamely, dragging themselves on that pursuit. Many hours of hardest toil had done their work. The wolf had vainly sought to fling them off. Now was his hour of doom, for he was spent; they still had some reserve. Straight to us for a time they came, skirting the base of the mountain, crawling.

We could not cross to join them, so held our breath and gazed with ravenous eyes. They were nearer now, the wind brought feeble notes from the hounds. The big wolf turned to the steep ascent, up a well known trail, it seemed, for he made no slip. My heart went with him, for he had come back to rescue his friend, and a momentary thrill of pity came over us both, as we saw him glance around and drag himself up the sloping way, to die on his mountain. There was no escape for him, beset by fifteen dogs with men to back. He was not walking, but tottering upward; the dogs behind in line, were now doing a little better, were nearing him. We could hear them gasping; we scarcely heard them bay— they had no breath for that; upward the grim procession went, circling a spur of the butte and along a ledge that climbed and narrowed, then dropped for a few yards to a shelf that reared above the canyon. The foremost dogs were closing, fearless of a foe so nearly spent.

Here in the narrowest place, where one wrong step meant death, the great wolf turned and faced them. With forefeet braced, with head low and tail a little raised, his dusky mane bristling, his glittering tusks laid bare, but uttering no sound that we could hear, he faced the

The great wolf turned and faced them.

crew. His legs were weak with toil, but his neck, his jaws, and his heart were strong, and—now all you who love the dogs had better close the book—on—up and down— fifteen to one, they came, the swiftest first, and how it was done, the eye could scarcely see, but even as a stream of water pours on a rock to be splashed in broken jets aside, that stream of dogs came pouring down the path, in a single file, and Duskymane received them as they came. A feeble spring, a counter lunge, a gash, and "Fango's down," has lost his foot hold and is gone. Dander and Coalie close and try to clinch; a rush, a heave, and they are fallen from that narrow path. Blue-spot then, backed by mighty Oscar and fearless Tige—but the wolf is next the rock and the flash of combat clears to show him there alone, the big dogs gone; the rest close in, the hindmost force the foremost on—down—to their death. Slash, chop and heave, from the swiftest to the biggest, to the last, down—down—he sent them whirling from the ledge to the gaping gulch below, where rocks and snags of trunks were sharp to do their work.

In fifty seconds it was done. The rock had splashed the stream aside—the Penroof pack was all wiped out, and Badlands Billy stood there alone again on his mountain.

A moment he waited to look for more to come. There were no more, the pack was dead, but waiting his breath, then raising his voice for the first time in that fatal scene, he feebly gave a long yell of triumph, and scaling the next low bank, was screened from view in a canyon of Sentinel Butte.

We stared like men of stone. The guns in our hands were forgotten. It was all so quick, so final. We made no move till the wolf was gone. It was not far to the place; we went on foot to see if any had escaped. Not one was left alive. We could do nothing, we could say nothing.

XI
The Howl at Sunset

A week later we were riding the upper trail back of the Chimney Pot, King and I. "The old man is pretty sick of it," he said. "He'd sell out if he could. He don't know what's the next move."

The sun went down beyond Sentinel Butte. It was dusk as we reached the turn that led to Dumont's place, and a deep-toned rolling howl came from the river flat below, followed by a number of higher pitched howls in answering chorus. We could see nothing, but we listened hard. The song was repeated, the hunting cry of the wolves. It faded, the night was stirred by another, the sharp bark and the short howl, the signal "close in;" a bellow came up, very short, for it was cut short.

And King as he touched his horse said grimly, "That's him, he is out with the pack, an' thar goes another beef."

Monarch
The Big Bear of Tallac

Seton saw a huge California grizzly named Monarch at the zoo at Golden Gate Park during a visit to San Francisco in August of 1899. He was appalled at the prison-like cage used to house the massive bear, and his sympathy toward it led him to investigate its history.

He discovered that the grizzly had been a known killer of cattle and sheep in the Tehachapi Range south of Bakersfield. It had been captured in 1889 by Allen Kelly, an editor of the *San Francisco Examiner*. Afterward, the bear was transported to the zoo in San Francisco.

Seton wrote in the foreword to his story about Monarch that he had gathered material from several witnesses who were familiar with the details of the bear's capture. For the early life history of the bear, Seton used information about several bears to draw a composite picture portraying the grizzly bear's youth. His goal was to describe typical grizzly behavior using Monarch, who was an exceptional individual, as the central character of the story. Because he took these liberties in telling the story, he described it as a "historical novel of Bear life."

Three years after Seton saw the great bear he returned to San Francisco and was pleased to find that Monarch had fathered two healthy cubs.

The reader will note Seton's unsympathetic portrayal of the Tampico brothers which reflects the Anglo-Saxon attitude toward Mexican-Americans prevalent at the time he wrote the story.

The story appeared in three parts in the *Ladies Home Journal* in the spring of 1904 and was later published in book form in 1907.

Monarch

The Big Bear of Tallac

I

The Two Springs

 High above Sierra's peaks stands grim Mount Tallac. Ten thousand feet above the sea it rears its head to gaze out north to the vast and wonderful turquoise that men call Lake Tahoe, and northwest, across a piney sea, to its great white sister, Shasta of the Snows; wonderful colors and things on every side, mast-like pine trees strung with jewelry, streams that a Buddhist would have made sacred, hills that an Arab would have held holy. But Lan Kellyan's keen grey eyes were turned to other things. The childish delight in life and light for their own sakes had faded, as they must in one whose training had been to make him hold them very cheap. Why value grass? All the world is grass. Why value air, when it is everywhere in measureless

immensity? Why value life, when, all alive, his living came from taking life? His senses were alert, not for the rainbow hills and the gem-bright lakes, but for the living things that he must meet in daily rivalry, each staking on the game, his life. Hunter was written on his leathern garb, on his tawny face, on his lithe and sinewy form and shone in his clear grey eye.

The cloven granite peak might pass unmarked, but a faint dimple in the sod did not. Calipers could not have told that it was widened at one end, but the hunter's eye did, and following, he looked for and found another, then smaller signs, and he knew that a big bear and two little ones had passed and were still close at hand, for the grass in the marks was yet unbending. Lan rode his hunting pony on the trail. It sniffed and stepped nervously, for it knew as well as the rider that a grizzly family was near. They came to a terrace leading to an open upland. Twenty feet on this side of it Lan slipped to the ground, dropped the reins, the well known sign to the pony that he must stand at that spot, then cocked his rifle and climbed the bank. At the top he went with yet greater caution, and soon saw an old grizzly with her two cubs. She was lying down some fifty yards away and afforded a poor shot; he fired at what seemed to be the shoulder. The aim was true, but the bear got only a flesh wound. She sprang to her feet and made for the place where the puff of smoke arose. The bear had fifty yards to cover, the man had fifteen, but she came racing down the bank before he was fairly on the horse, and for a hundred yards the pony bounded in terror while the old grizzly ran almost alongside, striking at him and missing by a scant hair's breath each time. But the grizzly rarely keeps up its great speed for many yards. The horse got under full headway, and the shaggy mother, falling behind, gave up the chase and returned to her cubs.

She was a singular old bear. She had a large patch of white on her breast, white cheeks and shoulders, graded into the brown elsewhere, and Lan from this remembered her afterward as the "Pinto." She had almost caught him that time, and the hunter was ready to believe that he owed her a grudge.

A week later his chance came. As he passed along the rim of Pocket Gulch, a small, deep valley with sides of sheer rock in most places, he saw afar the old Pinto Bear with her two little brown cubs. She was crossing

The pony bounded in terror while the grizzly ran almost alongside.

from one side where the wall was low to another part easy to climb. As she stopped to drink at the clear stream Lan fired with his rifle. At the shot Pinto turned on her cubs, and slapping first one, then the other, she chased them up a tree. Now a second shot struck her and she charged fiercely up the sloping part of the wall, clearly recognizing the whole situation and determined to destroy that hunter. She came snorting up the steep acclivity wounded and raging, only to receive a final shot in the brain that sent her rolling back to lie dead at the bottom of Pocket Gulch. The hunter, after waiting to make sure, moved to the edge and fired another shot into the old one's body; then reloading, he went cautiously down to the tree where still were the cubs. They gazed at him with wild seriousness as he approached them, and when he began to climb they scrambled up higher. Here one set up a plaintive whining and the other an angry growling, their outcries increasing as he came nearer.

He took out a stout cord, and noosing them in turn, dragged them to the ground. One rushed at him and, though little bigger than a cat, would certainly have done him serious injury had he not held it off with a forked stick. After tying them to a strong but swaying branch he went to his horse, got a grain bag, dropped them into that and rode with them to his shanty. He fastened each with a collar and chain to a post, up which they climbed, and sitting on the top they whined and growled, according to their humor. For the first few days there was danger of the cubs strangling themselves or of starving to death, but at length they were beguiled into drinking some milk most ungently procured from a range cow that was lassoed for the purpose. In another week they seemed somewhat reconciled to their lot, and thenceforth plainly notified their captor whenever they wanted food or water.

And thus the two small rills ran on, a little farther down the mountain now, deeper and wider, keeping near each other; leaping bars, rejoicing in the sunlight, held for a while by some trivial dam, but overleaping that and running on with pools and deeps that harbor bigger things.

II

The Springs and the Miner's Dam

Jack and Jill, the hunter named the cubs; and Jill, the little fury, did nothing to change his early impression of her bad temper. When at food time the man came she would get as far as possible up the post and growl, or else sit in sulky fear and silence; Jack would scramble down and strain at his chain to meet his captor, whining softly, and gobbling his food at once with the greatest of gusto and the worst of manners. He had many odd ways of his own, and he was a lasting rebuke to those who say an animal has no sense of humor. In a month he had grown so tame that he was allowed to run free. He followed his master like a dog, and his tricks and funny doings were a continual delight to Kellyan and the few friends he had in the mountains.

On the creek bottom below the shack was a meadow where Lan cut enough hay each year to feed his two ponies through the winter. This year when hay time came Jack was his daily companion, either following him about in dangerous nearness to the snorting scythe, or curling up an hour at a time on his coat to guard it assiduously from such aggressive monsters as ground squirrels and chipmunks. An interesting variation of the day came about whenever the mower found a bumblebee's nest. Jack loved honey, of course, and knew quite well what a bees' nest was, so the call, "Honey, Jacky, honey!" never failed to bring him in waddling haste to the spot. Jerking his nose up in token of pleasure, he would approach cautiously, for he knew that bees have stings. Watching his chance, he would dexterously slap at them with his paws till, one by one, they were knocked down and crushed; then sniffing hard for the latest information, he would stir up the nest gingerly till the very last was tempted forth to be killed. When the dozen or more that formed the swarm were thus got rid of, Jack would carefully dig out the nest and eat first the honey, next the grubs and wax, and last of all the bees he had killed, champing his jaws like a little pig at a trough, while his long red, snaky tongue was ever busy lashing the stragglers into his greedy maw.

Lan's nearest neighbor was Lou Bonamy, an ex-cowboy and sheepherder, now a prospecting miner. He lived with his dog in a shanty about a mile below Kellyan's shack. Bonamy had seen Jack "perform on a bee crew." And one day, as he came to Kellyan's, he called out, "Lan, bring Jack here, and we'll have some fun." He led the way down the stream into the woods. Kellyan followed him, and Jacky waddled at Kellyan's heels, sniffing once in a while to make sure he was not following the wrong pair of legs.

"There, Jacky, honey, honey!" and Bonamy pointed up a tree to an immense wasps' nest.

Jack cocked his head on one side and swung his nose on the other. Certainly those things buzzing about

"Honey — Jacky — honey."

looked like bees, though he never before saw a bees' nest of that shape or in such a place.

But he scrambled up the trunk. The men waited—Lan in doubt as to whether he should let his pet cub go into such danger, Bonamy insisting it would be a capital joke "to spring a surprise" on the little bear. Jack reached the branch that held the big nest high over the deep water, but went with increasing caution. He had never seen a bees' nest like this; it did not have the right smell. Then he took another step forward on the branch—what an awful lot of bees; another step—still they were undoubtedly bees; he cautiously advanced a foot—and bees mean honey; a little farther—he was now within four feet of the great paper globe. The bees hummed angrily and Jack stepped back, in doubt. The men giggled; then Bonamy called softly and untruthfully, "Honey, Jacky, honey!"

The little bear, fortunately for himself, went slowly, since in doubt; he made no sudden move, and he waited a long time, though urged to go on, till the whole swarm of bees had reentered their nest. Now Jacky jerked his nose up, hitched softly out a little farther till right over the fateful paper globe. He reached out, and by lucky chance put one horny little paw pad over the hole; his other arm grasped the nest, and leaping from the branch he plunged headlong into the pool below, taking the whole thing with him. As soon as he reached the water his hind feet were seen tearing into the nest, kicking it to pieces; then he let it go and struck out for the shore, the nest floating in rags down stream. He ran alongside till the comb lodged against a shallow place, then he plunged in again; the wasps were drowned or too wet to be dangerous, and he carried his prize to the bank in triumph. No honey; of course, that was a disappointment, but there were lots of fat white grubs—almost as good— and Jack ate till his paunch looked like a little rubber balloon.

"How is that?" chuckles Lan.

"The laugh is on us," answered Bonamy with a grimace.

Jack ate till his paunch looked like a rubber balloon.

III
The Trout Pool

Jack was now growing into a sturdy cub, and he would follow Kellyan even as far as Bonamy's shack. One day, as they watched him rolling head over heels in riotous glee, Kellyan remarked to his friend, "I'm afraid some one will happen on him an' shoot him in the woods for a wild b'ar."

"Then why don't you ear mark him with them thar new sheep rings?" was the sheep man's suggestion.

Thus it was that, much against his will, Jack's ears were punched and he was decorated with earrings like a prize ran. The intention was good, but they were neither ornamental nor comfortable. Jack fought them for days, and when at length he came home trailing a branch that was caught in the jewel of his left ear, Kellyan impatiently removed them.

At Bonamy's he formed two new acquaintances, a blustering, bullying old ram that was "in storage" for a sheep herder acquaintance, and which inspired him with a lasting enmity for everything that smelt of sheep— and Bonamy's dog.

This latter was an active, yapping, unpleasant cur that seemed to think it rare fun to snap at Jacky's heels, then bound out of reach. A joke is a joke, but this horrid beast did not know when to stop, and Jack's first and second visits to the Bonamy hut were quite spoiled by the tyranny of the dog. If Jack could have got hold of him he might have settled the account to his own satisfaction, but he was not quick enough for that. His only refuge was up a tree. He soon discovered that he was happier away from Bonamy's, and thenceforth when he saw his protector take the turn that led to the miner's cabin, Jack said plainly with a look, "No, thank you," and turned back to amuse himself at home.

His enemy, however, often came with Bonamy to the hunter's cabin, and there resumed his amusement of teasing the little bear. It proved so interesting a pursuit that the dog learned to come over on his own account whenever he felt like having some fun, until at length Jack was kept in continual terror of the yellow cur. But it all ended very suddenly.

One hot day, while the two men smoked in front of Kellyan's house, the dog chased Jack up a tree and then stretched himself out for a pleasant nap in the shade of its branches. Jack was forgotten as the dog slumbered. The little bear kept very quiet for a while, then, as his twinkling brown eyes came back to that hateful dog, that he could neither catch nor get away from, an idea seemed to grow in his small brain. He began to move slowly and silently down the branch until he was over the foe, slumbering, twitching his limbs, and making little sounds that told of dreams of the chase, or, more likely, dreams of tormenting a helpless bear cub. Of course, Jack knew nothing of that. His one thought, doubtless, was that he hated that cur and now he could vent his hate. He came just over the tyrant, and taking careful aim, he jumped and landed squarely on the dog's ribs. It was a terribly rude awakening, but the dog gave no yelp, for the good reason that the breath was knocked out of his body. No bones were broken, though he was barely able to drag himself away in silent defeat, while Jacky played a lively tune on his rear with paws that were fringed with meat hooks.

Evidently it was a most excellent plan; and when the dog came around after that, or when Jack went to Bonamy's with his master, as he soon again ventured to do, he would scheme with more or less success to "get the drop on the purp," as the men put it. The dog now rapidly lost interest in bear baiting, and in a short time it was a forgotten sport.

IV
The Stream that Sank in the Sand

Jack was funny; Jill was sulky. Jack was petted and given freedom, so grew funnier; Jill was beaten and chained, so grew sulkier. She had a bad name, and she was often punished for it; it is usually so.

One day, while Lan was away, Jill got free and joined her brother. They broke into the little storehouse and rioted among the provisions. They gorged themselves with the choicest sorts; and the common stuffs, like flour, butter, and baking powder, brought fifty miles on horseback, were good enough only to be thrown about the ground or rolled in. Jack had just torn open the last bag of flour, and Jill was puzzling over a box of miner's dynamite, when the doorway darkened and there stood Kellyan, a picture of amazement and wrath. Little bears do not know anything about pictures, but they have some acquaintance with wrath. They seemed to know that they were sinning, or at least in danger, and Jill sneaked, sulky and snuffy, into a dark corner, where she glared defiantly at the hunter. Jack put his head on one side, then, quite forgetful of all his misbehavior, he gave a delighted grunt, and scuttling toward the man, he whined, jerked his nose, and held up his sticky, greasy arms to be lifted and petted as though he were the best little bear in the world.

Jack . . . held up his sticky, greasy arms.

Alas, how likely we are to be taken at our own estimate! The scowl faded from the hunter's brow as the cheeky and deplorable little bear began to climb his leg. "You little devil," he growled, "I'll break your cussed neck;" but he did not. He lifted the nasty, sticky little beast and fondled him as usual, while Jill, no worse—even more excusable, because less trained—suffered all the terrors of his wrath and was double chained to the post, so as to have no further chance of such ill doing.

This was a day of bad luck for Kellyan. That morning he had fallen and broken his rifle. Now, on his return home, he found his provisions spoiled, and a new trial was before him.

A stranger with a small pack train called at his place that evening and passed the night with him. Jack was in his most frolicsome mood and amused them both with tricks half-puppy and half-monkey like, and in the morning, when the stranger was leaving, he said, "Say, pard, I'll give you twenty-five dollars for the pair." Lan hesitated, thought of the wasted provisions, his empty purse, his broken rifle, and answered, "Make it fifty and it's a go."

"Shake on it."

So the bargain was made, the money paid, and in fifteen minutes the stranger was gone with a little bear in each pannier of his horse.

Jill was surly and silent; Jack kept up a whining that smote on Lan's heart with a reproachful sound, but he braced himself with, "Guess they're better out of the way; couldn't afford another storeroom racket," and soon the pine forest had swallowed up the stranger, his three led horses, and the two little bears.

"Well, I'm glad he's gone," said Lan, savagely, though he knew quite well that he was already scourged with repentance. He began to set his shanty in order. He went to the storehouse and gathered the remnants of the provisions. After all, there was a good deal left. He walked past the box where Jack used to sleep. How silent it was! He noted the place where Jack used to scratch the door to get into the cabin, and started at the thought that he should hear it no more, and told himself, with many cuss words, that he was "mighty glad of it." He pottered about, doing—doing—oh, anything, for an hour or more; then suddenly he leaped on his pony and raced madly down the trail on the track of the stranger. He put the pony hard to it, and in two hours he overtook the train at the crossing of the river.

"Say, pard, I done wrong. I didn't orter sell them little b'ars, leastwise not Jacky. I—I—wall, now, I want to call it off. Here's yer yellow."

"I'm satisfied with my end of it," said the stranger coldly.

"Well, I ain't," said Lan, with warmth, "an' I want it off."

"Ye're wastin' time if that's what ye come for,' was the reply.

"We'll see about that," and Lan threw the gold pieces at the rider and walked over toward the pannier, where Jack was whining joyfully at the sound of the familiar voice.

"Hands up," said the stranger, with the short, sharp tone of one who had said it before, and Lan turned to find himself covered with a .45 Navy Colt.

"Ye got the drop on me," he said, "I ain't got no gun, but look-a here, stranger, that there little b'ar is the only pard I got; he's my stiddy company an' we're almighty fond o' each other. I didn't know how much I was a-goin' to miss him. Now look-here; take back yer fifty, ye give me Jack an' keep Jill."

"If ye got five hundred cold plunks in yaller ye kin get him; if not, you walk straight to that tree thar an' don't drop yer hands or turn or I'll fire. Now start."

Mountain etiquette is very strict, and Lan, being without weapons, must needs obey the rules. He marched to the distant tree under cover of the revolver. The wail of little Jack smote painfully on his ear, but he knew the ways of the mountaineers too well to turn or make another offer, and the stranger went on.

Many a man has spent a thousand dollars in efforts to capture some wild thing and felt it worth the cost, for a time. Then he is willing to sell it for half cost, then for a quarter, and at length he ends by giving it away. The stranger was vastly pleased with his comical bear cubs at first, and valued them proportionately; but each day they seemed more troublesome and less amusing, so that when, a week later, at the Bell Cross Ranch, he was offered a horse for the pair, he readily closed, and their days of hamper travel were over.

The owner of the ranch was neither mild, refined, nor patient. Jack, good natured as he was, partly grasped these facts as he found himself taken from the pannier, but when it came to getting cranky little Jill out of the basket and into a collar, there ensued a scene so unpleasant that no collar was needed. The rancher wore his hand in a sling for two weeks, and Jacky at his chain's end paced the ranch yard alone.

V
The River Held in the Foothills

There was little of pleasant interest in the next eighteen months of Jack's career. His share of the globe was a twenty-foot circle around a pole in the yard. The blue hills of the offing, the nearer pine grove, and even the ranch house itself were fixed stars, far away and sending merely faint suggestions of their splendors to his not very bright eyes. Even the horses and men were outside his little sphere and related to him about as much as comets are to the earth. The very tricks that had made him valued were being forgotten as Jack grew up in chains.

At first a butter firkin had made him an ample den, but he rapidly passed through the various stages—butter firkin, nail keg, flour barrel, oil barrel—and had now to be graded as a good average hogshead bear, though he was far from filling that big round wooden cavern that formed his latest den.

The ranch hotel lay just where the foothills of the Sierras with their groves of live oaks were sloping into the golden plains of the Sacramento. Nature had showered on it every wonderful gift in her lap. A foreground rich with flowers, luxuriant in fruit, shade and sun, dry pastures, rushing rivers, and murmuring rills, were here. Great trees were variants of the view, and the high Sierras to the east overtopped the wondrous plumy forests of their pines with blocks of sculptured blue. Back of the house was a noble river of water from the hills, fouled and chained by sluice and dam, but still a noble stream whose earliest parent rill had gushed from grim old Tallac's slope.

Things of beauty, life, and color were on every side, and yet most sordid of the human race were the folk about the ranch hotel. To see them in this setting might well raise doubt that any "rise from Nature up to Nature's God." No city slum has ever shown a more ignoble crew, and Jack, if his mind were capable of such things, must have graded the two-legged ones lower in proportion as he knew them better.

Cruelty was his lot, and hate was his response. Almost the only amusing trick he now did was helping himself to a drink of beer. He was very fond of beer, and the loafers about the tavern often gave him a bottle to see how dexterously he would twist off the wire and work out the cork. As soon as it popped, he would turn it up between his paws and drink to the last drop.

The monotony of his life was occasionally varied with a dog fight. His tormentors would bring their bear dogs "to try them on the cub." It seemed to be very pleasant sport to men and dogs, till Jack learned how to receive them. At first he used to rush furiously at the nearest tormentor until brought up with a jerk at the end of his chain and completely exposed to attack behind from another dog. A month or two entirely changed his method. He learned to sit against the hogshead and quietly watch the noisy dogs around him, with much show of inattention, making no move, no matter how near they were, until they bunched, that is, gathered in one place. Then he charged. It was inevitable that the hind dogs would be the last to jump, and so hindered the front ones; thus Jack would get one or more of them, and the game became unpopular.

When about eighteen months old, and half grown, an incident took place which defied all explanation. Jack had won the name of being dangerous, for he had crippled one man with a blow and nearly killed a tipsy fool who volunteered to fight him. A harmless but good-for-nothing sheep herder who loafed about the place got very drunk one night and offended some fire-eaters. They decided that, as he had no gun, it would be the proper thing to club him to their heart's content instead of shooting him full of holes, in the manner usually prescribed by their code. Faco Tampico made for the door and staggered out into the darkness. His pursuers were even more drunk, but, bent on mischief, they gave chase, and Faco dodged back of the house and into the yard. The mountaineers had just wit enough to keep out of reach of the grizzly as they searched about for their victim, but they did not find him. Then they got torches, and making sure that he was not in the yard, were satisfied that he had fallen into the river behind the barn and doubtless was drowned. A few rude jokes, and they returned to the house. As they passed the grizzly's den their lanterns awoke in his eyes a glint of fire. In the morning the cook, beginning his day, heard strange sounds in the yard. They came from the grizzly's den, "Hyar, you lay over dahr," in sleepy tones; then a deep, querulous grunting.

The cook went as close as he dared and peeped in. Said the same voice in sleepy tones, "Who are ye crowdin', caramba!" and a human elbow was seen jerking and pounding; and again impatient growling in bear-like tones was the response.

The sun came up, and the astonished loafers found it was the missing sheep herder that was in the bear's den, calmly sleeping off his debauch in the very cave of death. The men tried to get him out, but the grizzly plainly showed that they could do so only over his dead body. He charged with vindictive fury at any who ventured near, and when they gave up the attempt he lay down at the door of the den on guard. At length the sheep herder came to himself, rose up on his elbows, and realizing that he was in the power of the grizzly, he stepped gingerly over his guardian's back and ran off without even saying, "Thank you."

The Fourth of July was at hand now, and the owner of the tavern, growing weary of the huge captive in the yard, announced that he would celebrate

Independence Day with a grand fight between a "picked and fighting range bull and a ferocious Californian grizzly." The news was spread far and wide by the "Grapevine Telegraph." The roof of the stable was covered with seats at fifty cents each. The hay wagon was half-loaded and drawn alongside the corral; seats here gave a perfect view and were sold at a dollar apiece. The old corral was repaired, new posts put in where needed, and the first thing in the morning a vicious old bull was herded in and tormented till he was "snuffy" and extremely dangerous.

Jack meanwhile had been roped, choked down, and nailed up in his hogshead. His chain and collar were permanently riveted together, so the collar was taken off, as "it would be easy to rope him, if need be, after the bull was through with him."

The hogshead was rolled over to the corral gate and all was ready.

The cowboys came from far and near in their most gorgeous trappings, and the California cowboy is the peacock of his race. Their best girls were with them, and farmers and ranchmen came for fifty miles to enjoy the bull and bear fight. Miners from the hills were there, Mexican sheep herders, store keepers from Placerville, strangers from Sacramento; town and county, mountain and plain were represented. The hay wagon went so well that another was brought into market. The barn roof was sold out. An ominous crack of the timbers somewhat shook the prices, but a couple of strong uprights below restored the market, and all "The Corners" was ready and eager for the great fight. Men who had been raised among cattle were betting on the bull.

"I tell you, there ain't nothing on earth kin face a big range bull that hez good use of hisself."

But the hillmen were backing the bear. "Pooh, what's a bull to a grizzly? I tell you, I seen a grizzly send a horse clean over the Hetch-Hetchy with one clip of his left. Bull! I'll bet he'll never show up in the second round."

So they wrangled and bet, while burly women, trying to look fetching, gave themselves a variety of airs, were "scared at the whole thing, nervous about the uproar, afraid it would be shocking," but really were as keenly interested as the men.

All was ready, and the boss of "The Corners" shouted, "Let her go, boys; house is full an' time's up!"

Faco Tampico had managed to tie a bundle of 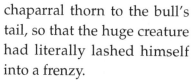 chaparral thorn to the bull's tail, so that the huge creature had literally lashed himself into a frenzy.

Jack's hogshead meanwhile had been rolled around till he was raging with disgust, and Faco, at the word of command, began to pry open the door. The end of the barrel was close to the fence, the door cleared away; now there was nothing for Jack to do but to go forth and claw the bull to pieces. But he did not go. The noise, the uproar, the strangeness of the crowd affected him so that he decided to stay where he was, and the bull-backers raised a derisive cry. Their champion came forward bellowing and sniffing, pausing often to paw the dust. He held his head very high and approached slowly until he came within ten feet of the grizzly's den; then, giving a snort, he turned and ran to the other end of the corral. Now it was the bear-backers turn to shout.

But the crowd wanted a fight, and Faco, forgetful of his debt to Grizzly Jack, dropped a bundle of Fourth of July crackers into the hogshead by way of the bung. "Crack!" and Jack jumped up. "Fizz—crack –c-r-r-r-a-a-c-k, cr-k-crk-ck!" and Jack in surprise rushed from his den into the arena. The bull was standing in a magnificent attitude there in the middle, but when he saw the bear spring toward him, he gave two mighty snorts and retreated as far as he could, amid cheers and hisses.

Perhaps the two main characteristics of the grizzly are the quickness with which he makes a plan and the vigor with which he follows it up. Before the bull had reached the far side of the corral Jack seemed to know the wisest of courses. His pig-like eyes swept the fence in a flash—took in the most climbable part, a place where a cross-piece was nailed on in the middle. In three seconds he was there, in two seconds he was over, and in one second he dashed through the running, scattering mob and was making for the hills as fast as his strong and supple legs could carry him. Women screamed, men yelled, and dogs barked; there was a wild dash for the horses tied far from the scene of the fight, to spare their nerves, but the grizzly had three hundred yards' start, five hundred yards even, and before the gala mob gave out a long and flying column of reckless, riotous riders, the grizzly had plunged into the river, a flood no dog cared to face, and had reached the chaparral and the broken ground in line for the piney hills. In an hour the ranch hotel, with its galling chain, its cruelties, and its brutal human beings, was a thing of the past, shut out by the hills of his youth, cut off by the river of his cub hood, the river grown from the rill born in his birth place away in Tallac's pines. That Fourth of July was a glorious Fourth—it was Independence Day for Grizzly Jack.

VI
The Broken Dam

A wounded deer usually works downhill, a hunted grizzly climbs. Jack knew nothing of the country, but he did know that he wanted to get away from that mob, so he sought the roughest ground, and climbed and climbed.

He had been alone for hours, traveling up and on. The plain was lost to view. He was among the granite rocks, the pine trees, and the berries now, and he gathered in food from the low bushes with dexterous paws and tongue as he traveled, but stopped not at all until among the tumbled rock, where the sun heat of the afternoon seemed to command rather than invite him to rest.

The night was black when he awoke, but bears are not afraid of the dark—they rather fear the day— and he swung along, led, as before, by the impulse to get up above the danger; and thus at last he reached the highest range, the region of his native Tallac.

He had but little of the usual training of a young bear, but he had a few instincts, his birthright, that stood him well in all the main issues, and his nose was an excellent guide. Thus he managed to live, and wild life experiences coming fast gave his mind the chance to grow.

Jack's memory for faces and facts was not at all good, but his memory for smells was imperishable. He had forgotten Bonamy's cur, but the smell of Bonamy's cur would instantly have thrilled him with the old feelings. He had forgotten the cross ram, but the smell of "Old Woolly Whiskers" would have inspired him at once with anger and hate; and one evening when the wind came richly laden with ram smell it was like a bygone life returned. He had been living on roots and berries for weeks and now began to experience that hankering for flesh that comes on every candid vegetarian with dangerous force from time to time. The ram smell seemed an answer to it. So down he went by night (no sensible bear travels by day), and the smell brought him from the pines on the hillside to an open rocky dale.

Long before he got there a curious light shone up. He knew what that was; he had seen the two-legged ones make it near the ranch of evil smells and memories, so feared it not. He swung along from ledge to ledge in silence and in haste, for the smell of sheep grew stronger at every stride, and when he reached a place above the fire he blinked his eyes to find the sheep. The smell was strong now; it was rank, but no sheep to be seen. Instead he saw in the valley a stretch of grey water that seemed to reflect the stars, and yet they neither twinkled nor rippled; there was a murmuring sound from the sheet, but it seemed not at all like that of the lakes around.

The stars were clustered chiefly near the fire, and were less like stars than spots of the phosphorescent wood that are scattered on the ground when one knocks a rotten stump about to lick up its swarms of wood ants. So Jack came closer, and at last so close that even his dull eyes could see. The great grey lake was a flock of sheep and the phosphorescent specks were their eyes. Close by the fire was a log or a low rough bank—that turned out to be the shepherd and his dog. Both were objectionable features, but the sheep extended far from them. Jack knew that his business was with the flock.

He came very close to the edge and found them surrounded by a low hedge of chaparral; but what little things they were compared with that great and terrible ram that he dimly remembered! The blood thirst came on him. He swept the low hedge aside; charged into the mass of sheep that surged away from him with rushing sounds of feet and murmuring groans, struck down one, seized it, and turning away, he scrambled back up the mountains.

The sheep herder leaped to his feet, fired his gun, and the dog came running over the solid mass of sheep, barking loudly. But Jack was gone. The sheep herder contented himself with making two or three fires, shooting off his gun and telling his beads.

That was Jack's first mutton, but it was not his last. Thenceforth when he wanted a sheep—and it became a regular need—he knew he had merely to walk along the ridge till his nose said, "Turn, and go so," for smelling is believing in bear life.

VII
The Freshet

Pedro Tampico and his brother Faco were not in the sheep business for any maudlin sentiment. They did not march ahead of their beloveds waving a crook as wand of office or appealing to the esthetic sides of their ideal followers with a tabret and pipe. Far from leading the flock with a symbol, they drove them with an armful of ever-ready rocks and clubs. They were not shepherds; they were sheep herders. They did not view their charges as loved and loving followers, but as four-legged cash; each sheep was worth a dollar bill. They were cared for only as a man cares for his money, and counted after each alarm or day of travel. It is not easy for any one to count three thousand sheep, and for a Mexican sheep herder it is an impossibility. But he had a simple device which answers the purpose. In an ordinary flock about one sheep in a hundred is a black one. If a portion of the flock has gone astray, there is likely to be a black one in it. So by counting his thirty black sheep each day Tampico kept rough count of his entire flock.

Grizzly Jack had killed but one sheep that first night. On his next visit he killed two, and on the next but one, yet that last one happened to be black, and when Tampico found but twenty-nine of its kind remaining he safely reasoned that he was losing sheep—according to the index a hundred were gone.

"If the land is unhealthy move out" is the ancient wisdom. Tampico filled his pocket with stones, and reviling his charges in all their walks in life and history, he drove them from the country that was evidently the range of a sheep-eater. At night he found a walled-in canyon, a natural corral, and the woolly scattering swarm, condensed into a solid fleece, went pouring into the gap, urged intelligently by the dog and idiotically by the man. At one side of the entrance Tampico made his fire. Some thirty feet away was a sheer wall of rock.

Ten miles may be a long day's travel for a wretched wool-plant, but it is little more than two hours for a grizzly. It is farther than eyesight, but it is well within nosesight, and Jack, feeling mutton-hungry, had not the lest difficulty in following his prey. His supper was a little later than usual, but his appetite was the better for that. There was no alarm in camp, so Tampico had fallen asleep. A growl from the dog awakened him. He started up to behold the most appalling creature that he had ever seen or imagined, a monster bear standing on his hind legs, and thirty feet high at least. The dog fled in terror, but was valor itself compared with Pedro. He was so frightened that he could not express the prayer that was in his breast, "Blessed saints, let him have every sin-blackened sheep in the band, but spare your poor worshiper," and he hid his head; so never learned that he saw, not a thirty-foot bear thirty feet away, but a seven-foot bear not far from the fire and casting a black thirty-foot shadow on the smooth rock behind. And, helpless with fear, poor Pedro groveled in the dust.

When he looked up the bear was gone. There was a rushing of the sheep. A small body of them scurried out of the canyon into the night, and after them went a ordinary-sized bear, undoubtedly a cub of the monster.

Pedro had been neglecting his prayers for some months back, but he afterward assured his father confessor that on this night he caught up on all arrears and had a goodly surplus before morning. At sunrise he left his dog in charge of the flock and set out to seek the

The thirty-foot bear.

runaways, knowing, first, that there was little danger in the daytime, second, that some would escape. The missing ones were a considerable number, raised to the second power indeed, for two more black ones were gone. Strange to tell, they had not scattered, and Pedro trailed them a mile or more in the wilderness till he reached another very small box canyon. Here he found the missing flock perched in various places on boulders and rocky pinnacles as high up as they could get. He was delighted and worked for half a minute on his bank surplus of prayers, but was sadly upset to find that nothing would induce the sheep to come down from the rocks or leave the canyon. One or two that he maneuvered as far as the outlet sprang back in fear from something on the ground, which, on examination, he found—yes, he swears to this—to be the deep-worn, fresh-worn pathway of a grizzly from one wall across to the other. All the sheep were now back again beyond his reach. Pedro began to fear for himself, so hastily returned to the main flock. He was worse off than ever now. The other grizzly was a bear of ordinary size and ate a sheep each night, but the new one, into whose range he had entered, was a monster, a bear mountain, requiring forty or fifty sheep to a meal. The sooner he was out of this the better.

It was now late, and the sheep were too tired to travel, so Pedro made unusual preparations for the night; two big fires at the entrance to the canyon, and a platform fifteen feet up in a tree for his own bed. The dog could look out for himself.

VIII
Roaring in the Canyon

Pedro knew that the big bear was coming; for the fifty sheep in the little canyon were not more than an appetizer for such a creature. He loaded his gun carefully as a matter of habit and went upstairs to bed. Whatever defects his dormitory had the ventilation was good and Pedro was soon a-shiver. He looked down in envy at his dog curled up by the fire; then he prayed that the saints might intervene and direct the steps of the bear toward the flock of some neighbor, and carefully specified the neighbor to avoid mistakes. He tried to pray himself to sleep. It had never failed in church when he was at the Mission, so why now? But for once it did not succeed. The fearsome hour of midnight passed, then the grey dawn, the hour of dull despair, was near. Tampico felt it, and a long groan vibrated through his chattering teeth. His dog leaped up, barked savagely, the sheep began to stir, then went backing into the gloom; there was a rushing of stampeding sheep and a huge, dark form loomed up. Tampico grasped his gun and would have fired, when it dawned on him with sickening horror that the bear was thirty feet high, his platform was only fifteen, just a convenient height for the monster. None but a madman would invite the bear to eat by shooting at him now. So Pedro flattened himself face downward on the platform, and, with his mouth to a crack, he poured forth prayers to his representative in the sky, regretting his unconventional attitude and profoundly hoping that it would be overlooked as unavoidable, and that somehow the petitions would get the right direction after leaving the under side of the platform.

In the morning he had proof that his prayers had been favorably received. There was a bear track, indeed, but the number of black sheep was unchanged, so Pedro filled his pocket with stones and began his usual torrent of remarks as he drove the flock.

"Hyah, Capitan—you huajalote," as the dog paused to drink. "Bring back those ill-descended sons of perdition," and a stone gave force to the order, which the dog promptly obeyed. Hovering about the great host of grumbling hoofy locusts, he kept them together and on the move, while Pedro played the part of a big, noisy, and troublesome second.

As they journeyed through the open country the sheep herder's eye fell on a human figure, a man sitting on a rock above them to the left. Pedro gazed inquiringly; the man saluted and beckoned. This meant "friend;" had he motioned him to pass on it might have meant, "Keep away or I shoot." Pedro walked toward him a little way and sat down. The man came forward. It was Lan Kellyan, the hunter.

Each was glad of a chance to "talk with a human" and to get the news. The latest concerning the price of wool, the bull and bear fiasco, and, above all, the monster bear that had killed Tampico's sheep, afforded topics of talk. "Ah, a bear devil—de hell-brute—a gringo bear—pardon, my amigo, I mean a very terror."

As the sheep herder enlarged on the marvelous cunning of the bear that had a private sheep corral of his own, and the size of the monster, forty or fifty feet high now—for such bears are of rapid and continuous growth—Kellyan's eye twinkled, and he said, "Say, Pedro, I believe you once lived pretty nigh the Hassayampa, didn't you?"

This does not mean that that is a country of great bears, but was an allusion to the popular belief that any one who tastes a single drop of the Hassayampa River can never afterward tell the truth. Some scientists who have looked into the matter aver that this wonderful property is common to the Rio Grande as well as the Hassayampa, and, indeed, all the rivers of Mexico, as well as their branches, and the springs, wells, ponds, lakes, and irrigation ditches. However that may be, the Hassayampa is the best known stream of this remarkable peculiarity. The higher one goes, the greater its potency, and Pedro was from the headwaters. But he protested by all the saints that his story was true. He pulled out a little bottle of garnets, got by glancing over the rubbish laid about their hills by the desert ants; he thrust it back into his wallet and produced another bottle with a small quantity of gold dust, also gathered at the rare times when he was not sleepy, and the sheep did not need driving, watering, stoning, or reviling.

"Here, I bet dat it ees so."

Gold is a loud talker.

Kellyan paused. "I can't cover your bet, Pedro, but I'll kill your bear for what's in the bottle."

"I take you," said the sheep herder, "eff you breeng back dose sheep dat are now starving up on de rocks of de canyon of Baxstaire's."

The Mexican's eyes twinkled as the white man closed on the offer. The gold in the bottle, ten or fifteen dollars, was a trifle, and yet enough to send the hunter on the quest—enough to lure him into the enterprise, and that was all that was needed. Pedro knew his man; get him going and profit would count for nothing; having put his hand to the plow Lan Kellyan would finish the furrow at any cost; he was incapable of turning back. And again he took up the trail of Grizzly Jack, his one-time pard, now grown beyond his ken.

The hunter went straight to Baxter's canyon and found the sheep high-perched upon the rocks. By the entrance he found the remains of two of them recently devoured, and about them the tracks of a medium-sized bear. He saw nothing of the pathway—the dead line—made by the grizzly to keep the sheep prisoners till he should need them. But the sheep were standing in stupid terror on various high places, apparently willing to starve rather then come down.

Lan drug one down; at once it climbed up again. He now realized the situation, so made a small pen of chaparral outside the canyon, and dragging the dull creatures down one at a time, he carried them—except one—out of the prison of death and into the pen. Next he made a hasty fence across the canyon's mouth, and turning the sheep out of the pen, he drove them by slow stages toward the rest of the flock.

Only six or seven miles across country, but it was late night when Lan arrived.

Tampico gladly turned over half of the promised dust. That night they camped together, and, of course, no bear appeared.

In the morning Lan went back to the canyon and found, as expected, that the bear had returned and killed the remaining sheep.

The hunter piled the rest of the carcasses in an open place, lightly sprinkled the grizzly's trail with some very dry brush, then making a platform some fifteen feet from the ground in a tree, he rolled up in his blanket there and slept.

An old bear will rarely visit a place three nights in succession; a cunning bear will avoid a trail that has been changed overnight; a skillful bear goes in absolute silence. But Jack was neither old, cunning, nor skillful. He came for the fourth time to the canyon of the sheep. He followed his old trail straight to the delicious mutton bones. He found the human trail, but there was something about it that rather attracted him. He strode along on the dry boughs. "Crack!" went one; "crack-crack!" went another; and Kellyan arose on the platform and strained his eyes in the gloom till a dark form moved into the opening by the bones of the sheep. The hunter's rifle cracked, the bear snorted, wheeled into the bushes, and, crashing away, was gone.

IX
Fire and Water

That was Jack's baptism of fire, for the rifle had cut a deep flesh wound in his back. Snorting with pain and rage, he tore through the bushes and traveled on for an hour or more, then lay down and tried to lick the wound, but it was beyond reach. He could only rub it against a log. He continued his journey back toward Tallac, and there, in a cave that was formed of tumbled rocks, he lay down to rest. He was still rolling about in pain when the sun was high and a strange smell of fire came searching through the cave; it increased, and volumes of blinding smoke were about him. It grew so choking that he was forced to move, but it followed him till he could bear it no longer, and he dashed out of another of the ways that led into the cavern. As he went he caught a distant glimpse of a man throwing wood on the fire by the in-way, and the whiff that the wind brought him said, "This is the man that was last night watching the sheep." Strange as it may seem, the woods were clear of smoke except for a trifling belt that floated in the trees, and Jack went striding away in peace. He passed over the ridge, and finding berries, ate the first meal he had known since killing his last sheep. He had wandered on, gathering fruit and digging roots, for an hour or two, when the smoke grew blacker, the smell of fire stronger. He worked away from it, but in no haste. The birds, deer, and wood hares were now seen scurrying past him. There was a roaring in the air. It grew louder, was coming nearer, and Jack turned to stride after the wood things that fled.

The whole forest was ablaze; the wind was rising, and the flames, gaining and spreading, were flying now like wild horses. Jack had no place in his brain for such a thing; but his instinct warned him to shun that coming roaring that sent above dark clouds and flying fire flakes, and messengers of heat below, so he fled before it, as the forest host was doing. Fast as he went, and few animals can outrun a grizzly in rough country, the hot hurricane was gaining on him. His sense of danger had grown almost to terror, terror of a kind that he had never known before, for here there was nothing he could fight; nothing that he could resist. The flames were all around him now;

birds without number, hares, and deer had gone down before the red horror. He was plunging wildly on through chaparral and manzanita thickets that held all feebler things until the fury seized them; his hair was scorching, his wound was forgotten, and he thought only of escape when the brush ahead opened, and the grizzly, smoke-blinded, half-roasted, plunged down a bank and into a small clear pool. The fur on his back said "hiss," for it was sizzling hot. Down below he went, gulping the cool drink, wallowing in safety and unheat. Down below the surface he crouched as long as his lungs would bear the strain, then slowly and cautiously he raised his head. They sky above was one great sheet of flame. Sticks aflame and flying embers came in hissing showers on the water. The air was hot, but breathable at times, and he filled his lungs till he had difficulty in keeping his body down below. Other creatures there were in the pool, some burnt, some dead, some small and in the margin, some bigger in the deeper places, and one of them was close beside him. Oh, he knew that smell; fire—all Sierra's woods ablaze—could not disguise the hunter who had shot at him from the platform, and, though he did not know this, the hunter really who had followed him all day, and who had tried to smoke him out of his den and thereby set the woods ablaze.

Here they were, face to face, in the deepest end of the little pool; they were only ten feet apart and could not get more than twenty feet apart. The flames grew unbearable. The bear and man each took a hasty breath and bobbed below the surface, each wondering, according to his intelligence, what the other would do. In half a minute both came up again, each relieved to find the other no nearer. Each tried to keep his nose and one eye above the water. But the fire was raging hot; they had to dip under and stay as long as possible.

The roaring of the flame was like a hurricane. A huge pine tree came crashing down across the pool; it barely missed the man. The splash of water quenched the blazes for the most part, but it gave off such a heat that he had to move—a little nearer to the bear. Another fell at an angle, killing a coyote, and crossing the first tree. They blazed fiercely at their junction, and the bear edged from it a little nearer the man. Now they were within touching distance. His useless gun was lying in shallow water near shore, but the man had his knife ready, ready for self defense. It was not needed; the fiery power had proclaimed a peace. Bobbing up and dodging under, keeping a nose in the air and eye on his foe, each spent an hour or more. The red hurricane passed on. The smoke was bad in the woods, but no longer intolerable,

and as the bear straightened up in the pool to move away into shallower water and off into the woods, the man got a glimpse of red blood streaming from the shaggy back and dyeing the pool. The blood on the trail had not escaped him. He knew that this was the bear of Baxter's canyon, this was the Gringo Bear, but he did not know that this was also his old-time Grizzly Jack. He scrambled out of the pond, on the other side from that taken by the grizzly, and, hunter and hunted, they went their diverse ways.

X
The Eddy

All the west slopes of Tallac were swept by the fire, and Kellyan moved to a new hut on the east side, where still were green patches; so did the grouse and the rabbit and the coyote, and so did Grizzly Jack. His wound healed quickly, but his memory of the rifle smell continued; it was a dangerous smell, a new and horrible kind of smoke—one he was destined to know too well; one, indeed, he was soon to meet again. Jack was wandering down the side of Tallac, following a sweet odor that called up memories of former joys—the smell of honey, though he did not know it. A flock of grouse got leisurely out of his way and flew to a low tree, when he caught a whiff of man smell, then heard a crack like that which had stung him in the sheep corral, and down fell one of the grouse close beside him. He stepped forward to sniff just as a man also stepped forward from the opposite bushes. They were within ten feet of each other, and they recognized each other, for the hunter saw that it was a singed bear with a wounded side, and the bear smelt the rifle smoke and the leather clothes. Quick as a grizzly—that is, quicker than a flash—the bear reared. The man sprang backward, tripped and fell, and the grizzly was upon him. Face to earth the hunter lay like dead, but, ere he struck, Jack caught a scent that made him pause. He smelt his victim, and the smell was the rolling back of curtains or the conjuring up of a past. The days in the hunter's shanty were forgotten, but the feelings of those days were ready to take command at the bidding of the nose. His nose drank deep of a draft that quelled all rage. The grizzly's humor changed. He turned and left the hunter quite unharmed.

Oh, blind one with the gun! All he could find in explanation was, "You kin never tell what a grizzly will do, but it's good play to lay low when he has you cornered." It never came into his mind to credit the shaggy brute with an impulse born of good, and when he told the sheep herder of his adventure in the pool, of his hitting high on the body and of losing the trail in the forest fire—"down by the shack, when he turned up sudden and had me, I thought my last day was come. Why he didn't swat me, I don't know. But I tell you this, Pedro, the b'ar what killed your sheep on the upper pasture in the sheep canyon is the same. No two b'ars has hind feet alike when you get a clear cut track, and this holds out even right along."

"What about the fifty-foot b'ar I saw wit' mine own eyes, caramba?"

"That must have been the night you were working a kill-care with your sheep herder's delight. But don't worry, I'll get him yet."

So Kellyan set out on a long hunt, and put in practice every trick he knew for the circumventing of a bear. Lou Bonamy was invited to join with him, for his yellow cur was trailer. They packed four horses with stuff and led them over the ridge to the east side of Tallac, and down away from Jack's Peak, that Kellyan had named in honor of his bear cub, toward Fallen Leaf Lake. The hunter believed that here he would meet not only the Gringo Bear that he was after, but would also stand a chance of finding others, for the place had escaped the fire.

They quickly camped, setting up their canvas sheet for shade more than against rain, and, after picketing their horses in a meadow, went out to hunt. By circling around Leaf Lake they got a good idea of the wild population: plenty of deer, some black bear, and one or two cinnamon and grizzly, and one track along the shore that Kellyan pointed to, briefly saying, "That's him."

"Ye mean old Pedro's Gringo?"

"Yep. That's the fifty-foot grizzly. I suppose he stands maybe seven foot high in daylight, but, 'course, b'ars pulls out long at night."

So the yellow cur was put on the track, and led away with funny little yelps, while the two hunter came stumbling along behind him as fast as they could, calling, at times, to the dog not to go so fast, and thus making a good deal of noise, which Gringo Jack heard a mile away as he ambled along the mountain side above them. He was following his nose to many good and eatable things, and therefore going up wind. This noise behind was so peculiar that he wanted to smell it, and to do that he swung long back over the clamor, then descended to the down wind side, and thus he came on the trail of the hunters and their dog.

His nose informed him at once. Here was the hunter he once felt kindly toward and two other smells of far back—both hateful; all three were now the smell-marks of foes, and a rumbling "woof" was the expressive sound that came from his throat.

That dog smell in particular aroused him, though it is very sure he had forgotten all about the dog, and Gringo's feet went swiftly and silently, yes, with marvelous silence, along the tracks of the enemy.

On rough, rocky ground a dog is scarcely quicker than a bear, and since the dog was constantly held back by the hunter the bear had no difficulty in overtaking them. Only a hundred yards or so behind he continued, partly in curiosity, pursuing the dog that was pursuing him, till a shift of the wind brought the dog a smell-call from the bear behind. He wheeled—of course you never follow trail smell when you can find body smell—and came galloping back with a different yapping and a bristling in his mane.

"Don't understand that," whispered Bonamy.

"It's b'ar, all right," was the answer, and the dog, bounding high, went straight toward the foe.

Jack heard him coming, smelt him coming, and at length saw him coming, but it was the smell that roused him—the full scent of the bully of his youth. The anger of those days came on him, and cunning enough to make him lurk in ambush; he backed to one side of the trail where it passed under a root, and, as the little yellow tyrant came, Jack hit him once, hit him as he had done some years before, but now with the power of a grown grizzly. No yelp escaped the dog, no second blow was needed. The hunters searched in silence for half an hour before they found the place and learned the tale from many silent tongues.

"I'll get even with him," muttered Bonamy, for he loved that contemptible little yap-cur.

"That's Pedro's Gringo, all right. He's sure cunning to run his own back track. But we'll fix him yet," and they vowed to kill that bear or "get done up" themselves.

Without a dog, they must make a new plan of hunting. They picked out two or three good places for pen traps, where trees stood in pairs to make the pillars of the den. Then Kellyan returned to camp for the ax while Bonamy prepared the ground.

As Kellyan came near their open camping place, he stopped from habit and peeped ahead for a minute. He was about to go down when a movement caught his eye. There, on his haunches, sat a grizzly, looking down on the camp. The singed brown of his head and neck, and the white spot on each side of his back, left no doubt that Kellyan and Pedro's Gringo were again face to face. It was a long shot, but the rifle went up, and as he was about to fire, the bear suddenly bent his head down, and lifting his hind paw, began to lick at a little cut. This brought the head and chest nearly in line with Kellyan—sure shot; so sure that he fired hastily. He missed the head and the shoulder, but, strange to say, he hit the bear in the mouth and in the hind toe, carrying away one of his teeth and the side of one toe. The grizzly sprang up with a snort, and came tearing down the hill toward the hunter. Kellyan climbed a tree and got ready, but the camp lay just between them, and the bear charged on that instead. One sweep of his paw and the canvas tent was down and torn. Whack! And tins went flying this way. Whick! And flour sacks went that. Rip! And the flour went off like smoke. Slap—crack! And a boxful of odds and ends was scattered into the fire. Whack! And a bagful of cartridges was tumbled after it. Whang! And the water pail was crushed. Pat-pat-pat! And all the cups were in useless bits.

Kellyan, safe up the tree, got no fair view to shoot—could only wait till the storm center cleared a little. The bear chanced on a bottle of something with a cork loosely in it. He seized it adroitly in his paws, twisted out the cork, and held the bottle up to his mouth with a comical dexterity that told of previous experience. But, whatever it was, it did not please the invader; he spat and spilled it out, and flung the bottle down as Kellyan gazed, astonished. A remarkable "crack! crack! crack!" from the fire was heard now, and the cartridges began to go off in ones, twos, fours, and numbers unknown. Gringo whirled about; he had smashed everything in view. He did not like that Fourth of July sound, so, springing to a bank, he went bumping and heaving down to the meadow and had just stampeded the horses when, for the first time, Gringo exposed himself to the hunter's aim. His flank was grazed by another leaden stinger, and Gringo, wheeling, went off into the woods.

The hunters were badly defeated. It was fully a week before they had repaired all the damage done by their shaggy visitor and were once more at Fallen Leaf Lake with a new store of ammunition and provisions, their tent repaired, and their camp outfit complete. They said little about their vow to kill that bear. Both took for granted that it was a fight to the finish. They never said, "If we get him," but, "When we get him."

XI
The Ford

Gringo, savage, but still discreet, scaled the long mountain side when he left the ruined camp, and afar on the southern slope he sought a quiet bed in a manzanita thicket, there to lie down and nurse his wounds and rest his head so sorely aching with the jar of his shattered tooth. There he lay for a day and a night,  sometimes in great pain, and at no time inclined to stir. But, driven forth by hunger on the second day, he quit his couch and, making for the nearest ridge, he followed that and searched the wind with his nose. The smell of a mountain hunter reached him. Not knowing just what to do he sat down and did nothing. The smell grew stronger, he heard sounds of trampling; closer they came, then the brush parted and a man on horseback appeared. The horse snorted and tried to wheel, but the ridge was narrow and one false step might have been serious. The cowboy held his horse in hand and, although he had a gun, he made no attempt to shoot at the surly animal blinking at him and barring his path. He was an old mountaineer, and he now used a trick that had long been practiced by the Indians, from whom, indeed, he learned it. He began "making medicine with his voice."

"See here now, b'ar," he called aloud. "I ain't doing nothing to you. I ain't got no grudge ag'in' you, an' you ain't got no right to a grudge ag'in' me."

"Gro-o-o-h," said Gringo, deep and low.

"Now, I don't want no scrap with you, though I have my scrap-iron right handy, an' what I want you to do is just step aside an' let me pass that narrer trail an' go about business."

"Grow-woo-oo-wow," grumbled Gringo.

"I'm honest about it pard. You let me alone, and I'll let you alone; all I want is right of way for five minutes."

"Grow-grow-wow-oo-umph," was the answer.

"Ye see, thar's no way round an' on'y one way through, an' you happen to be settin' in it. I got to take it, for I can't turn back. Come, now, is it a bargain—hands off and no scrap?"

Now, B'ar, I don't want no scrap with you.

It is very sure that Gringo could see in this nothing but a human making queer, unmenacing, monotonous sounds, so giving a final "Gr-u-ph," the bear blinked his eyes, rose to his feet and strode down the bank, and the cowboy forced his unwilling horse to and past the place.

"Wall, wall," he chuckled, "I never knowed it to fail. Thar's whar most b'ars is alike."

If Gringo had been able to think clearly, he might have said, "This surely is a new kind of man."

XII
Swirl and Pool and Growing Flood

Gringo wandered on with nose alert, passing countless odors of berries, roots, grouse, deer, till a new and pleasing smell came with especial force.

It was not sheep, or game, or a dead thing. It was a smell of living meat. He followed the guide to a little meadow, and there he found it. There were five of them, red, or red and white—great things as big as himself; but he had no fear of them. The hunter instinct came on him, and the hunter's audacity and love of achievement. He sneaked toward them upwind in order that he might still smell them, and it also kept them from smelling him. He reached the edge of the wood. Here he must stop or be seen. There was a watering place close by. He silently drank, then lay down in a thicket where he could watch. An hour passed thus. The sun went down, and the cattle arose to graze. One of them, a small one, wandered nearer, then, acting suddenly with purpose, walked to the water hole. Gringo watched his chance, and as she foundered in the mud and stooped, he reared and struck with all his force. Square at her skull he aimed, and the blow went straight. But Gringo knew nothings of horns. The young, sharp horn upcurling, hit his foot and was broken off; the blow lost half its power. The beef went down, but Gringo had to follow up the blow, then raged and tore in anger for his wounded paw. The other cattle fled from the scene. The grizzly took the heifer in his jaws, then climbed the hill to his lair, and with this store of food he again lay down to nurse his wounds. Though painful, they were not serious, and within a week or so Grizzly Jack was as well as ever and roaming the woods about Fallen Leaf Lake and farther south and east, for he was extending his range as he grew—the king was coming to his kingdom. In time he met others of his kind and matched his strength with theirs. Sometimes he won and sometimes lost, but he kept on growing as the months went by, growing and learning and adding to his power.

Kellyan had kept track of him and knew at least the main facts of his life, because he had one or two marks that always served to distinguish him. A study of the tracks had told of the round wound in the front foot and the wound in the hind foot. But there was another; the hunter had picked up the splinters of bone at the camp where he had fired at the bear, and, after long doubt, he guessed that he had broken a tusk. He hesitated to tell the story of hitting a tooth and hind toe at the same shot till, later, he had clearer proof of its truth.

No two animals are alike. Kinds which herd have more sameness than those that do not, and the grizzly, being a solitary kind, shows great individuality. Most grizzlies mark their length on the trees by rubbing their backs, and some will turn on the tree and claw it with their fore paws; others hug the tree with their fore paws and rake it with their hind claws. Gringo's peculiarity of marking was to rub first, then turn and tear the trunk with his teeth.

It was on examining one of the bear trees one day that Kellyan discovered the facts. He had been tracking the bear all morning, had a fine set of tracks in the dusty trail, and thus learned that the rifle wound was a toe shot in the hind foot, but his fore foot of the same side had a large round wound, the one really made by the cow's horn. When he came to the bear tree where Gringo had carved his initials, the marks were clearly made by the bear's teeth, and one of the upper tusks was broken off, so the evidence of identity was complete.

"It's the same old b'ar," said Lan to his pard.

They failed to get sight of him in all this time, so the partners set to work at a series of bear traps. These are made of heavy logs and have a sliding door of hewn planks. The bait is on a trigger at the far end; a tug on this lets the door drop. It was a week's hard work to make four of these traps. They did not set them at once, for no bear will go near a thing so suspiciously new looking. Some bears will not approach one till it is weather beaten and grey. But they removed all chips and covered they newly cut wood with mud, then rubbed the inside with stale meat, and hung a lump of ancient venison on the trigger of each trap.

They did not go around for three days, knowing that the human smell must first be dissipated, and then they found but one trap sprung, the door down. Bonamy became greatly excited, for they had crossed the grizzly's track close by. But Kellyan had been studying the dust and suddenly laughed aloud.

"Look at that," he pointed to a thing like a bear track, but scarcely two inches long. "There's the b'ar we'll find in that; that's a bushy-tailed b'ar," and Bonamy joined in the laugh when he realized that the victim in the big trap was nothing but a little skunk.

"Next time we'll set the bait higher and not set the trigger so fine."

They rubbed their boots with stale meat when they went the rounds, then left the traps for a week.

There are bears that eat little but roots and berries; there are bears that love best the great black salmon they can hook out of the pools when the long run is on; and there are bears that have a special fondness for flesh. These are rare; they are apt to develop unusual ferocity and meet an early death. Gringo was one of them, and he grew like the brawny, meat-fed gladiators of old—bigger, stronger, and fiercer than his fruit and root-fed kin. In contrast with this was his love of honey. The hunter on his trail learned that he never failed to dig out any bees' nest he could find, or, finding none, he would eat the little honey flowers that hung like sleigh bells on the heather. Kellyan was quick to mark the signs. "Say, Bonamy, we've got to find some honey."

It is not easy to find a bee tree without honey to fill your bee-guides; so Bonamy rode down the mountain to the nearest camp, the Tampico sheep camp, and got not honey but some sugar, of which they made syrup. They caught bees at three or four different places, tagged them with cotton, filled them with syrup and let them fly, watching till the cotton tufts were lost to view, and by going on the lines till they met they found the hive. A piece of gunny sack filled with comb was put on each trigger, and that night, as Gringo strode with that long, untiring swing that eats up miles like steam wheels, his sentinel nose reported the delicious smell, the one that above the rest meant joy. So Gringo Jack followed fast and far, for the place was a mile away, and reaching the curious log cavern, he halted and sniffed. There were hunters' smells; yes, but, above all, that smell of joy. He walked around to be sure, and knew it was inside; then cautiously he entered. Some wood mice scurried by. He sniffed the bait, licked it, mumbled it, slobbered it, reveled in it, tugged to increase the flow, when "bang!" went the great door behind and Jack was caught. He backed up with a rush, bumped into the door, and had a sense, at least, of peril. He turned over with an effort and attacked the door, but it was strong. He examined the pen; went all around the logs where their rounded sides seemed easiest to tear at with his teeth. But they yielded nothing. He tried them all; he tore at the roof, the floor; but all were heavy, hard logs, spiked and pinned as one.

The sun came up as he raged, and shone through the little cracks of the door, and so he turned all his power on that. The door was flat, gave little hold, but he battered with his paws and tore with his teeth till plank after plank gave way. With a final crash he drove the wreck before him, and Jack was free again.

The men read the story as though in print; yes, better, for bits of plank can tell no lies, and the track to the pen and from the pen was the track of a big bear with a cut on the hind foot and a curious round peg-like scar on the front paw, while the logs inside, where little torn, gave proof of a broken tooth.

"We had him that time, but he knew too much for us. Never mind, we'll see."

So they kept on and caught him again, for honey he could not resist. But the wreckage of the trap was all they found in the morning.

Pedro's brother knew a man who had trapped bears, and the sheep herder remembered that it is necessary to have the door quite light-tight rather than very strong , so they battened all with tar paper outside. But Gringo was learning pen-traps. He did not break the door that he did not see through, but he put one paw under and heaved it up when he had finished the bait. Thus he baffled them and sported with the traps, till Kellyan made the door drop into a deep groove so that the bear could put no claw beneath it. But it was cold weather now. There was deepening snow on the Sierras. The bear sign disappeared. The hunters knew that Gringo was sleeping his winter's sleep.

XIII
The Deepening Channel

April was bidding high Sierra snows go back to Mother Sea. The California woodwales screamed in clamorous joy. They thought it was about a few acorns left in storage in the Live Oak bark, but it was really joy of being alive. This outcry was to them what music is to the thrush, what joy bells are to us—a great noise to tell how glad they were. The deer were bounding, grouse were booming, rills were rushing—all things were full of noisy gladness.

Kellyan and Bonamy were back on the grizzly quest. "Time he was out again, and good trailing to get him, with lots of snow in the hollows." They had come prepared for a long hunt. Honey for bait, great steel traps with crocodilian jaws, and guns there were in the outfit. The pen-trap, the better for the aging, was repaired and rebaited, and several black bears were taken. But Gringo, if about, had learned to shun it.

He was about, and the men soon learned that. His winter sleep was over. They found the peg print in the snow, but with it, or just ahead, was another, the tracks of a small bear.

"See that," and Kellyan pointed to the smaller mark. "This is mating time; this is Gringo's honeymoon," and he followed the trail for while, not expecting to find them, but simply to know their movements. He followed several times and for miles, and the trail told him many things. Here was the track of a third bear joining. Here were marks of combat, and a rival driven away was written there, and then the pair went on. Down from the rugged hills it took him once to where a love feast had been set by the bigger bear; for the carcass of a steer lay half devoured, and the telltale ground said much of the struggle that foreran the feast. As though to show his power, the bear had seized the steer by the nose and held him for while— so said the trampled earth for rods—struggling, bellowing, no doubt, music for my lady's ears, till Gringo judged it time to strike him down with paws of steel.

Once only the hunters saw the pair - a momentary glimpse of a bear so huge they half believed Tampico's tale, and a bear of lesser size in fur that rolled and rippled in the sun with brown and silver lights.

"Oh, ain't that just the beautifulest thing that ever walked!" and both the hunters gazed as she strode from view in the chaparral. It was only a neck of the thicket; they both must reappear in a minute at the other side, and the men prepared to fire; but for some incomprehensible reason the two did not appear again. They never quit the cover, and had wandered far away before the hunters knew it, and were seen of them no more.

But Faco Tampico saw them. He was visiting his brother with the sheep, and hunting in the foot hills to the eastward, in hopes of getting a deer, his small black eyes fell on a pair of bears, still love-bound, roaming in the woods. They were far below him. He was safe, and he sent a ball that laid the bear low; her back was broken. She fell with a cry of pain and vainly tried to rise. Then

Gringo rushed around, sniffed the wind for the foe, and Faco fired again. The sound and the smoke puff told Gringo where the man lay hid. He raged up the cliff, but Faco climbed a tree, and Gringo went back to his mate. Faco fired again. Gringo made still another effort to reach him, but could not find him now, so returned to his "Silver-brown."

Whether it was chance or choice can never be known, but when Faco fired once more, Gringo Jack was between, and the ball struck him. It was the last in Faco's pouch, and the grizzly, charging as before, found not a trace of the foe. He was gone—had swung across a place no bear could cross and soon was a mile away. The big bear limped back to his mate, but she no longer responded to his touch. He watched about for a time, but no one came. The silvery hide was never touched by man, and when the semblance of his mate was gone, Gringo quit the place.

The world was full of hunters, traps, and guns. He turned toward the lower hills where the sheep grazed, where once he had raided Pedro's flocks, limping along, for now he had another flesh wound. He found the scent of the foe that killed his "Silver-brown," and would have followed, but it ceased at a place where a horse track joined. Yet he found it again that night, mixed with the sheep smell so familiar once. He followed this, sore and savage. It led him to a settler's flimsy shack, the house of Tampico's parents, and as the big bear reached it, two human beings scrambled out of the rear door.

"My husband," shrieked the woman, "pray! Let us pray to the saints for help!"

"Where is my pistol?" cried the husband.

"Trust in the saints." said the frightened woman.

"Yes, if I had a cannon or if this was a cat; but with only a pepper box pistol to meet a bear mountain, it is better to trust to a tree," and old Tampico scrambled up a pine.

The grizzly looked into the shack, then passed to the pig pen, killed the largest there, for this was a new kind of meat, and carrying it off, he made his evening meal.

He came again and again to that pig pen. He found his food there till his wound was healed. Once he met with a spring-gun, but it was set too high. Six feet up, the sheep folk judged, would be just about right for such a bear; the charge went over his head, and so he passed unharmed—a clear proof that he was a devil. He was learning this; the human smell in any form is a smell of danger. He quit the little valley of the shack, wandering downward toward the plains. He passed a house one night, and walking up, he discovered a hollow thing with a delicious smell. It was a ten gallon keg that had been used for sugar, some of which was still in the bottom, and thrusting in his huge head, the keg rim, bristling with nails, stuck to him. He raged about, clawing at it wildly and roaring in it until a charge of shot from the upper windows stirred him to such effort that the keg was smashed to bits and his blinders removed.

Thus the idea was slowly borne in on him; going near a man-den is sure to bring trouble. Thenceforth he sought his prey in the woods or on the plains. He one day found the man scent that enraged him the day he lost his "Silver-brown." He took the trail, and passing in silence incredible for such a bulk, he threaded chaparral and manzanita on and down through tule beds till the level plain was reached. The scent led on, was fresher now. Far out were white specks, moving things. They meant nothing to Gringo, for he had never smelt wild geese, had scarcely seen them, but the trail he was hunting went on. He swiftly followed till the tule ahead rustled gently, and the scent was body scent. A ponderous rush, a single blow, and the goose hunt was ended ere well begun, and Faco's sheep became the brother's heritage.

XIV
The Cataract

"What is next, Lan?" said Lou, as they sat dispirited by the fire that night. Kellyan was silent for a time, then said slowly and earnestly, with a gleam in his eye, "Lou, that's the greatest bear alive. When I seen him set up there like a butte and swat horses like they was flies, I jest loved him. He's the greatest thing God has turned loose in these yer hills. Before today, I sure wanted to get him; now, Lou, I'm a-going to get him, an' get him alive, if it takes all my natural days. I think I kin do it alone, but I know I kin do it with you," and deep in Kellyan's eyes there glowed a little spark of something not yet rightly named.

They were camped in the hills, being no longer welcome at the ranch; the ranchers thought their price too high. Some even decided that the Monarch, being a terror to sheep, was not an undesirable neighbor. The cattle bounty was withdrawn, but the newspaper bounty was not.

"I want you to bring in that bear," was the brief but pregnant message from the rich newsman when he heard of the fight with the riders.

"How are you going about it, Lan?"

Every bridge has its rotten plank, every fence its flimsy rail, every great one his weakness, and Kellyan, as he pondered, knew how mad it was to meet this one of brawn with mere brute force.

"Steel traps are no good; he smashes them. Lariats won't do, and he knows all about log traps. But I have a scheme. First, we must follow him up and learn his range. I reckon that'll take three months."

So the two kept on. They took up the bear trail next day; they found the lariats chewed off. They followed day after day. They learned what they could from rancher and sheep herder, and much more was told them than they could believe.

Three months, Lan said, but it took six months to carry out his plan; meanwhile Monarch killed and killed.

In each section of his range they made cage traps of bolted logs. At the back end of each they put a small grating of heavy steel bars. The door was carefully made and fitted into grooves. It was of double plank, with tar paper between to make it surely light-tight. It was sheeted with iron on the inside, and when it dropped it went into an iron-bound groove in the floor.

They left these traps open and unset till they were greyed with age and smelt no more of man. Then the two hunters prepared for the final play. They baited all without setting them—baited them with honey, the lure that Monarch never had refused—and when at length they found the honey baits were gone, they came where he now was taking toll and laid the long planned snare. Every trap was set, and baited as before with a mass of honey—but honey now mixed with a potent sleeping draft.

XV
The Foaming Flood

Just as fads will for a time sway human life, so crazes may run through all animals of a given kind. This was the year when a beef-eating craze seemed to possess every able-bodied Grizzly of the Sierras. They had long been known as a root-eating, berry-picking, inoffensive race when let alone, but now they seemed to descend on the cattle range in a body and make their diet wholly of flesh.

One cattle outfit after another was attacked, and the whole country seemed divided up among bears of incredible size, cunning, and destructiveness. The cattlemen offered bounties, very large bounties at last, but still the bears kept on. Very few were killed, and it became a kind of rude jest to call each section of the range, not by the cattle brand, but by the grizzly that was quartered on its stock.

Wonderful tales were told of these various bears of the new breed. The swiftest was Reelfoot, the Placerville cattle-killer that could charge from a thicket thirty yards away and certainly catch a steer before it could turn and run, and that could even catch ponies in the open when they were poor. The most cunning of all was Brin, the Mokelumne Grizzly that killed by preference blooded stock, would pick out a Merino ram or a white-faced Hereford from among fifty grades; that killed a new beef every night; that never again returned to it, or gave the chance for traps or poisoning.

The Pegtrack Grizzly of Feather River was rarely seen by any. He was enveloped in mysterious terror. He moved and killed by night. Pigs were his favorite food, and he had also killed a number of men.

But Pedro's Grizzly was the most marvelous. "Hassayampa," as the sheep herder was dubbed, came one night to Kellyan's hut.

"I tell you he's still dere. He has keel me a t'ousand sheep. You telled me you keel heem; you haff not. He is beegare as dat tree. He eat only sheep—much sheep. I tell you he ees Gringo devil—he ees devil bear. I haff three cows, two fat, one theen. He catch and keel de fat; de lean run off. He roll een dust—make great dust. Cow come for see what make dust; he catch her an' keel. My fader got bees. De devil bear chaw pine; I know he by hees broke toof. He gum hees face and nose wit' pine gum so bees no sting, then eat all bees. He devil all time. He get much rotten manzanita and eat till drunk—locoed—then go crazy and keel sheep just for fun. He get beeg bull by nose and drag like rat for fun. He keel cow, sheep, and keel Faco too, for fun. He devil. You promise me you keel heem; you nevaire keel."

This is a condensation of Pedro's excited account. And there was yet one more—the big bear that owned the range from the Stanislaus to the Merced, the "Monarch of the Range" he had been styled. He was believed—yes, known to be—the biggest bear alive, a creature of supernatural intelligence. He killed cows for food, and scattered sheep or conquered bulls for pleasure.

It was even said that the appearance of an unusually big bull anywhere was a guarantee that Monarch would be there for the joy of combat with a worthy foe. A destroyer of cattle, sheep, pigs, and horses, and yet a creature known only by his track. He was never seen, and his nightly raids seemed planned with consummate skill to avoid all kinds of snares.

The cattlemen clubbed together and offered an enormous bounty for every grizzly killed in the range. Bear trappers came and caught some bears, brown and cinnamon, but the cattle killing went on. They set out better traps of massive steel and iron bars, and at length they caught a killer, the Mokelumne Grizzly; yes, and read in the dust how he had come at last and made the fateful step; but steel will break and iron will bend. The great bear trail was there to tell the tale; for a while he had raged and chafed at the hard black reptile biting into his paw; then, seeking a boulder, he had released the paw by smashing the trap to pieces on it. Thenceforth each year he grew more cunning, huge, and destructive.

Kellyan and Bonamy came down from the mountains now, tempted by the offered rewards. They saw the huge tracks; they learned that cattle were not killed in all places at once. They studied and hunted. They got at length in the dust the full impressions of the feet of the various monsters in regions wide apart, and they saw that all the cattle were killed in the same way—their muzzles torn, their necks broken; and last, the marks on the trees where the bears had reared and rubbed, then scored them with a broken tusk, the same all through the wide range; and Kellyan told them with calm certainty, "Pedro's Gringo, Old Pegtrack, the Placerville Grizzly, and the Monarch of the Range are one and the same bear."

The little man from the mountains and the big man from the hills set about the task of hunting him down with an intensity of purpose which, like the river that is dammed, grew more fierce from being balked.

All manner of traps had failed for him. Steel traps he could smash, no log trap was strong enough to hold this furry elephant; he would not come to a bait; he never fed twice from the same kill.

Two reckless boys once trailed him to a rocky glen. The horses would not enter; the boys went in on foot, and were never seen again. The Mexicans held him in superstitious terror, believing that he could not be killed; and he passed another year in the cattle land, known and feared now as the "Monarch of the Range," killing in the open by night, and retiring by day to his fastness in the near hills, where horsemen could not follow.

Bonamy had been called away; but all that summer and winter, too,—for the grizzly no longer "denned up,"—Kellyan rode and rode, each time too late or too soon to meet the Monarch. He was almost giving up, not in despair, but for lack of means, when a message came from a rich man, a city journalist, offering to multiply the reward by ten if, instead of killing the Monarch, he would bring him in alive.

Kellyan sent for his old partner, and when word came that the previous night three cows were killed in the familiar way near the Bell Dash pasture, they spared neither horse nor man to reach the spot. A ten-hour ride by night meant worn-out horses, but the men were iron, and new horses with scarcely a minute's delay were brought to them. Here were the newly killed beeves, there the mighty footprints with the scars that spelled his name. No hound could have tracked him better than Kellyan did. Five miles away from the foot of the hills was an impenetrable thicket of chaparral. The great tracks went in, did not come out, so Bonamy sat sentinel while Kellyan rode back with the news. "Saddle up the best we got!" was the order. Rifles were taken down and cartridge belts being swung when Kellyan called a halt.

"Say, boys, we've got him safe enough. He won't try to leave the chapparral till night. If we shoot him we get the cattlemen's bounty; if we take him alive, an' it's easy in the open, we get the newspaper bounty, ten times as big. Let's leave all guns behind; lariats are enough."

"Why not have the guns along to be handy?"

"'Cause I know the crowd too well; they couldn't resist the chance to let him have it; so no guns at all. It's ten to one on the riata."

Nevertheless three of them brought their heavy revolvers. Seven gallant riders on seven fine horses, they rode out that day to meet the Monarch of the Range. He was still in the thicket, for it was yet morning. They threw stones in and shouted to drive him out, without effect, till the noon breeze of the plains arose, the down current of air from the hills. Then they fired the grass in several places, and it sent a rolling sheet of flame and smoke into the thicket. There was a crackling louder than the fire, a smashing of brush, and from the farther side out hurled the Monarch Bear, the Gringo, Grizzly Jack. Horsemen were all about him now, armed not with guns but with the rawhide snakes whose loops in air spell bonds or death. The men were calm, but the horses were snorting and plunging in fear. This way and that the grizzly looked up at the horsemen—a little bit; scarcely up at the horses; then turning without haste, he strode toward the friendly hills.

"Look out, now, Bill! Manuel! It's up to you."

Oh, noble horses, nervy men! Oh, grand old grizzly, how I see you now! Cattle keepers and cattle killer face to face!

Three riders of the range that horse had never thrown were sailing, swooping, like falcons; their lariats swung, sang—sang higher—and Monarch, much perplexed, but scarcely angered yet, rose to his hind legs, then from his towering height looked down on horse and man. If, as they say, the vanquished prowess goes into the victor, then surely in that mighty chest, those arms like necks of bulls, was the power of the thousand cattle he had downed in fight.

"Caramba! What a bear! Pedro was not so far astray,"

"Sing—sing—sing!" the lariats flew. "Swish—pat!" One, two, three, they fell. These were not men to miss. Three ropes, three horses, leaping away to bear on the great beast's neck. But swifter than thought the supple paws went up. The ropes were slipped, and the spurred cowponies, ready for the shock, went, shockless, bounding, loose ropes trailing afar.

"Hi—Hal! Ho—Lan! Head him!" as the grizzly, liking not the unequal fight, made for the hills. But a deft Mexican in silver gear sent his hide riata whistling, then haunched his horse as the certain coil sank in the grizzly's hock, and checked the Monarch with a heavy jar. Uttering one great snort of rage, he turned; his huge jaws crossed the rope, back nearly to his ears it went, and he ground it as a dog might grind a twig, so the straining pony bounded free.

Round and round him now the riders swooped, waiting their chance. More than once his neck was caught, but he slipped the noose as though it were all play. Again he was caught by a foot and wrenched, almost thrown, by the weight of two strong steeds, and now he foamed in rage. Memories of olden days, or more likely the habit of olden days, came on him, days when he learned to strike the yelping pack that dodged his blows. He was far from the burnt thicket, but a single bush was near, and setting his broad back to that, he waited for the circling foe. Nearer and nearer they urged the frightened steeds, and Monarch watched, waited, as of old, for the dogs till they were almost touching each other, then he sprang like an avalanche of rock. What can elude a grizzly's dash? The earth shivered as he launched himself and trembled when he struck. Three men, three horses, in each other's way. The dust was thick; they only knew he struck—struck—struck! The horses never rose.

"Santa Maria!" came a cry of death, and hovering riders dashed to draw the bear away. Three horses dead, one man dead, one nearly so, and only one escaped.

"Crack! crack! crack!" went the pistols now as the bear went rocking his huge form in rapid charge for the friendly hills; and the four riders, urged by Kellyan, followed fast. They passed him, wheeled, faced him. The pistols had wounded him in many places.

"Don't shoot, don't shoot, but tire him out," the hunter urged.

"Tire him out? Look at Carlos and Manuel back there. How many minutes will it be before the rest are down with them?" So the infuriating pistols popped till all their shots were gone, and Monarch foamed with slobbering jaws of rage.

"Keep on! Keep cool," cried Kellyan.

His lariat flew as the cattle-killing paw was lifted for an instant. The lasso bound his wrist. "Sing! Sing!" went two, and caught by the neck. A bull with his great

Rumbling and snorting, he made for the friendly hills.

club foot in a noose is surely caught, but the grizzly raised his supple, hand-like, tapering paw and gave one jerk that freed it. Now the two on his neck were tight; he could not slip them. The horses at the ends were dragging, choking him; men were shouting, hovering, watching for a new chance, when Monarch, firmly planting both paws, braced, bent those mighty shoulders, and, spite of shortening breath, leaned back on those two ropes as Samson did on pillars of the house of Baal, and straining horses with their riders were dragged forward more and more, long grooves being plowed behind; dragging them, he backed faster and faster still. His eyes were starting, his tongue lolling out.

"Keep on! Hole tight!" was the cry, till the ropers swung together, the better to resist; and Monarch, big and strong with frenzied hate, seeing now his turn, sprang forward like a shot. The horses leaped and escaped, almost; the last was one small inch too slow. The awful paw with jags of steel just grazed his flank. How slight it sounds! But what it really means is better not written down.

The riders had slipped their ropes in fear, and the Monarch, rumbling, snorting, bounding, trailed them to the hills, there to bite them off in peace, while the remnant of the gallant crew went, sadly muttering, back.

Bitter words went round. Kellyan was cursed.

"His fault. Why didn't we have the guns?"

"We were all in it," was the answer, and more hard words, till Kellyan flushed, forgot his calm, and drew a pistol hitherto concealed, and the other "took it back."

XVI
Landlocked

That night the great bear left his lair, one of his many lairs, and, cured of all his wounds, rejoicing in the fullness of his mighty strength, he strode toward the plains. His nose, ever alert, reported—sheep, a deer, a grouse, men, more sheep, some cows, and some calves; a bull—a fighting bull—and Monarch wheeled in big, rude bearish joy at the coming battle brunt; but as he hugely hulked from hill to hill a different message came, so soft and low, so different from the smell of beefish brutes, one might well wonder he could sense it, but like a tiny ringing bell when thunder booms it came, and Monarch wheeled at once. Oh, it cast a potent spell! It stood for something very near to ecstasy with him, and down the hill and through the pines he went, on and on faster yet, abandoned to its sorcery. Here to its home he traced it, a long, low cavern. He had seen such many times before, had been held in them more than once, but had learned to spurn them. For weeks he had been robbing them of their treasures, and its odor, like a calling voice, was still his guide. Into the cavern he passed and it reeked with the smell of joy. There was the luscious mass, and Monarch, with all caution lulled now, licked and licked, then seized to tear the bag for more, when down went the door with a low bang. The Monarch started, but all was still and there was no smell of danger. He had forced such doors before. His palate craved the honey still, and he licked and licked, greedily at first, then calmly, then slowly, then drowsily, then at last stopped. His eyes were closing, and he sank slowly down on the earth and slept a heavy sleep.

Calm, but white-faced, were they—the men—when in the dawn they came. There were the huge scarred tracks leading in; there was the door down; there dimly they could see a mass of fur that filled the pen, that heaved in deepest sleep.

Strong ropes, strong chains and bands of steel were at hand, with chloroform, lest he should revive too soon. Through holes in the roof with infinite toil they chained him, bound him, his paws to his neck, his neck and breast and hind legs to a bolted beam. Then raising the door, they dragged him out, not with horses—none would go near—but with a windlass to a tree; and fearing the sleep of death, they let him now revive.

Chained and double-chained, frenzied, foaming, and impotent, what words can tell the state of the fallen Monarch? They put him on a sled, and six horses with a long chain drew it by stages to the plain, to the railway. They fed him enough to save his life. A great steam derrick lifted bear and beam and chain on to a flatcar, a tarpaulin was spread above his helpless form; the engine puffed, pulled out; and the Grizzly King was gone from his ancient hills.

So they brought him to the great city, the Monarch born, in chains. They put him in a cage not merely strong enough for a lion, but thrice as strong, and once a rope gave way as the huge one strained his bonds. "He is loose," went the cry, and an army of onlookers and keepers fled; only the small man with the calm eye and the big man of the hills were stanch, so the Monarch was still held.

Free in the cage, he swung round, looked this way and that, then heaved his powers against the triple angling steel and wrenched the cage so not a part of it was square. In time he clearly would break out. They dragged the prisoner to another that an elephant could not break down, but it stood on the ground, and in an hour the great beast had a cavern into the earth and was sinking out of sight, till a stream of water sent after him filled the hole and forced him again to view. They moved him to a new cage made for him since he came—a hard rock floor, great bars of nearly two inch steel that reached up nine feet and then projected in for five. The Monarch wheeled once around, then, rearing, raised his ponderous bulk, wrenched those bars, unbreakable, and bent and turned them in their sockets with one heave till the five foot spears were pointed out, and then sprang to climb. Nothing but spikes and blazing brands in a dozen ruthless hands could hold him back. The keepers watched him night and day till a stronger cage was made, impregnable with a steel above and rocks below.

The Untamed One passed swiftly around, tried every bar, examined every corner, sought for a crack in the rocky floor, and found at last the place where was a six inch timber beam, the only piece of wood in its frame. It was sheathed in iron, but exposed for an inch its whole length. One claw could reach the wood, and here he lay on his side and raked, raked all day till a great pile of shavings was lying by it and the beam sawn in two; but the cross bolts remained, and when Monarch put his vast shoulder to the place it yielded not a whit. That was his last hope; now it was gone; and the huge bear sank down in the cage with his nose in his paws and sobbed long, heavy sobs, animal sounds indeed, but telling just as truly as in man of the broken spirit, the hope and the life gone out. The keepers came with food at the appointed time, but the bear moved not. They set it down, but in the morning it was still untouched. The bear was lying as before, his ponderous form in the pose he had first taken. The sobbing was replaced by a low moan at intervals.

Two days went by. The food, untouched, was corrupting in the sun. The third day, and Monarch still lay on his breast, his huge muzzle under his huger paw. His eyes were hidden; only a slight heaving of his broad chest was now seen.

"He is dying," said one keeper. "He can't live overnight."

"Send for Kellyan," said another.

So Kellyan came, slight and thin. There was the beast that he had chained, pining, dying. He had sobbed his life out in his last hope's death, and a thrill of pity came over the hunter, for men of grit and power love grit and power. He put his arm through the cage bars and stroked him, but Monarch made no sign. His body was cold. At length a little moan was sign of life, and Kellyan said, "Here, let me go in to him."

"You are mad," said the keepers, and they would not open the cage. But Kellyan persisted till they put in a cross-grating in front of the bear. Then, with this between, he approached. His hand was on the shaggy head, but Monarch lay as before. The hunter stroked his victim and spoke to him. His hand went to the big round ears, small above the head. They were rough to his touch. He looked again, then started. What! Is it true? Yes, the stranger's tale was true, for both ears were pierced with a round hole, one torn large, and Kellyan knew that once again he had met his little Jack.

"Why, Jacky, I didn't know it was you. I never would have done it if I had known it was you. Jacky, old pard, don't you know me?"

But Jack stirred not, and Kellyan got up quickly. Back to the hotel he flew; there he put on his hunter's suit, smoky and smelling of pine gum and grease, and returned with a mass of honeycomb to reenter the cage.

"Jacky, Jacky! he cried, "honey, honey!" and he held the tempting comb before him. But Monarch lay as one dead now.

"Jacky, Jacky! Don't you know me?" He dropped the honey and laid his hands on the great muzzle.

The voice was forgotten. The old time invitation, "Honey, Jacky, honey," had lost its power, but the smell of the honey, the coat, the hands that he had fondled, had together a hidden potency.

There is a time when the dying of our race forget their life, but clearly remember the scenes of childhood; these only are real and return with master power. And why not with a bear? The power of scent was there to call them back again, and Jacky, the Grizzly Monarch, raised his head a little, just a little; the eyes were nearly closed, but the big brown nose was jerked up feebly two or three times, the sign of interest that Jacky used to give in days of old. Now it was Kellyan that broke down even as the bear had done.

"I didn't know it was you, Jacky, or I never would have done it. Oh, Jacky, forgive me!" He rose and fled from the cage.

The keepers were there. They scarcely understood the scene, but one of them, acting on the hint, pushed the honeycomb nearer and cried, "Honey, Jacky, honey!"

Filled by despair, he had lain down to die, but here was a new-born hope, not clear, not exact as words might put it, but his conqueror had shown himself a friend; this seemed a new hope, and the keeper, taking up the old call, "Honey, Jacky, honey!" pushed the comb till it touched his muzzle. The smell was wafted to his sense, its message reached his brain; hope honored, it must wake response. The great tongue licked the comb, appetite revived, and thus in new-born hope began the chapter of his gloom.

Skillful keepers were there with plans to meet the Monarch's every want. Delicate foods were offered and every shift was tried to tempt him back to strength and prison life.

He ate and—lived.

And still he lives, but pacing, pacing, pacing, you may see him, scanning not the crowds, but something beyond the crowds, breaking down at times into petulant rages, but recovering his ponderous dignity, looking, waiting, watching, held ever by that hope, that unknown hope, that came. Kellyan has been to him since, but Monarch knows him not. Over his head, beyond him, was the great bear's gaze, far away toward Tallac or far away on the sea, we knowing not which or why, but pacing, pacing, pacing, held like the storied Wandering One to a life of ceaseless journey, a journey aimless, endless, and sad.

The wound spots long ago have left his shaggy coat, but the earmarks still are there, the ponderous strength, the elephantine dignity. His eyes are dull, never were bright, but they seem not vacant, and most often fixed on the Golden Gate where the river seeks the sea.

The river, born in high Sierra's flank, that lived and rolled and grew, through mountain pines, overleaping man-made barriers, then to reach with growing power the plains and bring its mighty flood at last to the Bay of Bays, a prisoner there to lie, the prisoner of the Golden Gate, seeking forever Freedom' Blue, seeking and raging—raging and seeking—back and forth, forever—in vain.

285

Coaly-Bay,
The Outlaw Horse

eton and his wife Grace went on a pack trip in the Bitteroot Range on the Montana-Idaho border in summer of 1902. The trip was arranged by W. J. Leeds, a rancher from Hamilton, Montana and was guided by his brother, Abe, who was a well-known bear hunter of the surrounding mountain country. On return from the trip, Seton wrote in his journal that he considered the Bitterroots the roughest mountain range he had ever been in.

After leaving horseback from Leeds' ranch and passing into Idaho, Abe Leeds picked up an outlaw horse on another ranch that he wanted to use as bait to capture a bear. The bay horse had a mean disposition and was unbroken to ride. Consequently, he was destined to be slaughtered in order to entice grizzly bears into traps.

Seton' story about the horse appeared in the January issue of *Collier's* in 1916 and in his book, *Wild Animal Ways*. Coaly-Bay shared many characteristics with the actual horse, including being able to fake lameness. The major difference was that Coaly-Bay was successful in escaping from his human enemies while the bay horse was killed for the purpose intended.

Coaly-Bay,
The Outlaw Horse

The Wilful Beauty

 Years ago in the Bitterroot Mountains of Idaho there was a beautiful little foal. His coat was bright bay; his legs, mane, and tail were glossy black—coal black and bright bay—so they named him Coaly-bay.

"Coaly-bay" sounds like "Koli-bey," which is an Arab title of nobility, and those who saw the handsome colt, and did not know how he came by the name, thought he must be of Arab blood. No doubt he was, in a faraway sense; just as all of our best horses have Arab blood, and once in a while it seems to come out strong and show in every part of the creature, in his frame, his power, and his wild, free roving spirit.

Coaly-bay loved to race like the wind, he gloried in his speed, his tireless legs, and when careering with the herd of colts they met a fence or ditch, it was as natural to Coaly-bay to overleap it, as it was for the others to sheer off.

So he grew up strong of limb, restless of spirit, and rebellious at any thought of restraint. Even the kindly curb of the hay yard or the stable was unwelcome, and he soon showed that he would rather stand out all night in a driving storm than be locked in a comfortable stall where he had no vestige of the liberty he loved so well.

He became very clever at dodging the horse wrangler whose job it was to bring the horse herd to the corral. The very sight of that man set Coaly-bay a going. He became what is known as "Quit-the bunch"—that is a horse of such independent mind that he will go his own way the moment he does not like the way of the herd.

So each month the colt became more set on living free, and more cunning in the means he took to win his way. Far down in his soul, too, there must have been a streak of cruelty, for he stuck at nothing and spared no one that seemed to stand between him and his one desire.

When he was three years of age, just in the perfection of his young strength and beauty, his real troubles began, for now his owner undertook to break him to ride. He was as tricky and vicious as he was handsome, and the first day's experience was a terrible battle between the horse trainer and the beautiful colt.

But the man was skillful. He knew how to apply his power, and all the wild plunging, bucking, rearing, and rolling of the wild one had no desirable result. With all his strength the horse was hopelessly helpless in the hands of the skillful horseman, and Coaly-bay was so far mastered at length that a good rider could use him. But each time the saddle went on, he made a new fight. After a few months of this the colt seemed to realize that it was useless to resist, it simply won for him lashings and spurings, so he pretended to reform. For a week he was ridden each day and not once did he buck, but on the last day he came home lame.

His owner turned him out to pasture. Three days later he seemed all right; he was caught and saddled. He did not buck, but within five minutes he went lame as before. Again he was turned out to pasture, and after a week, saddled, only to go lame again.

His owner did not know what to think, whether the horse really had a lame leg or was only shamming, but he took the first chance to get rid of him, and though

Coaly-bay was easily worth fifty dollars, he sold him for twenty five. The new owner felt he had a bargain, but after being ridden half a mile Coaly-bay went lame. The rider got off to examine the foot, whereupon Coaly-bay broke away and galloped back to his old pasture. Here he was caught, and the new owner, being neither gentle or sweet, applied spur without mercy, so that the next twenty miles was covered in less than two hours and no sign of lameness appeared.

Now they were at the ranch of this new owner. Coaly-bay was led from the door of the house to the pasture, limping all the way, and then turned out. He limped over to the others horses. On one side of the pasture was the garden of a neighbor. This man was very proud of his fine vegetables and had put a six foot fence around the place. Yet the very night after Coaly-bay arrived, certain of the horses got into the garden

somehow and did a great deal of damage. But they leaped out before daylight and no one saw them.

The gardener was furious, but the ranchman stoutly maintained that it must have been some other horses, since his were behind a six foot fence.

Next night it happened again. The ranchman went out very early and saw all his horses in the pasture with Coaly-bay behind them. His lameness seemed worse now instead of better. In a few day, however, the horse was seen walking all right, so the ranchman's son caught him and tried to ride him. But his seemed too good a chance to lose; all his old wickedness returned to the horse; the boy was bucked off at once and hurt. The ranchman himself now leaped into the saddle; Coaly-bay bucked for ten minutes, but finding he could not throw the man, he tried to crush his leg against a post, but the rider guarded himself well. Coaly-bay reared and threw himself backward; the rider slipped off, the horse fell, jarring heavily, and before he could rise the man was in the saddle again. The horse now ran away, plunging and bucking; he stopped short, but the rider did not go over his head, so Coaly-bay turned, seized the man's foot in his teeth, and but for heavy blows on the nose would have torn him dreadfully. It was quite clear now that Coaly-bay was an "outlaw"—that is an incurable vicious horse.

The saddle was jerked off, and he was driven, limping, into the pasture.

The raids on the garden continued, and the two men began to quarrel over it. But to prove that his horses were not guilty the ranchman asked the gardener to sit up with him and watch. That night as the moon was brightly shining they saw, not all the horses, but Coaly-bay, walk straight up to the garden fence—no sign of a limp now—easily leap over it, and proceed to gobble the finest things he could find. After they had made sure of his identity, the men ran forward. Coaly-bay cleared the fence like a deer, lightly raced over the pasture to mix with the horse herd, and when the men came near him he had—oh, such an awful limp.

"That settles it," said the rancher. "He's a fraud, but he's a beauty, and good stuff, too."

"Yes, but it settles who took my garden truck," said the other.

"Wall, I suppose so," was the answer; "but luk a here, neighbor, you ain't lost more'n ten dollars in truck. That horse is easily worth—a hundred. Give me twenty five dollars, take the horse, an' call it square."

"Not much I will," said the gardener. "I'm out twenty five dollars worth of truck; the horse ain't worth a cent more. I take him and call it even."

And so the thing was settled. The ranchman said nothing about Coaly-bay being vicious as well as cunning, but the gardener found out the very first time he tried to ride that the horse was as bad as he was beautiful.

Next day a sign appeared on the gardener's gate"

> FOR SALE — First-class
> horse, sound and gentle.
> $10.00

The Bear Bait

Now at this time a band of hunters came riding by. There were three mountaineers, two men from the city, and the writer of this story. The city men were going to hunt bear. They had guns and everything needed for bear hunting, except bait. It is usual to buy some worthless horse or cow, drive it into the mountains where the bears are, and kill it there. So seeing the sign up, the hunters called to the gardener, "Haven't you got a cheaper horse?"

The gardener replied, "Look at him there, ain't he a beauty? You won't find a cheaper horse if you travel a thousand miles."

"We are looking for an old bear bait, and five dollars is our limit," replied the hunter.

Horses were cheap and plentiful in that country; buyers were scarce. The gardener feared that Coaly-bay would escape. "Wall, if that's the best you can do, he's yourn."

The hunter handed him five dollars, then said, "Now, stranger, bargain's settled. Will you tell me why you sell this fine horse for five dollars?"

"Mighty simple. He can't be rode. He's dead lame when he's going your way and sound as a dollar going his own; no fence in the country can hold him; he's a dangerous outlaw. He's wickeder than old Nick."

"Well, he's an almighty handsome bear bait," and the hunters rode on.

Coaly-bay was driven with the pack horses and limped dreadfully on the trail. Once or twice he tried to go back, but he was easily turned by the men behind him. His limp grew worse, and toward night it was painful to see him.

The leading guide remarked, "That thar limp ain't no fake. He's got some deep seated trouble."

Day after day the hunters rode farther into the mountains, driving the horses along and hobbling them at night. Coaly-bay went with the rest, limping along, tossing his head and his long splendid mane at every step. One of the hunters tried to ride him and nearly lost his life, for the horse seemed possessed of a demon as soon as the man was on his back.

The road grew harder as it rose. A very bad bog had to be crossed one day. Several horses were mired in it, and as the men rushed to the rescue, Coaly-bay saw his chance of escape. He wheeled in a moment and turned himself from a limping, low-headed, sorry, bad-eyed creature into a high spirited horse. Head and tail aloft now, shaking their black streamers in the wind, he gave a joyous neigh, and, without a trace of lameness, dashed for his home one hundred miles away, threading each narrow trail with perfect certainty, though he had seen them but once before, and in a few minutes he had steamed away from their sight.

The men were furious, but one of them, saying not a word, leaped on his horse—to do what? Follow that free ranging racer? Sheer folly. Oh, no!—he knew a better plan. He knew the country. Two miles around by the trail, half a mile by the rough cut- off that he took, was Panther Gap. The runaway must pass through that, and Coaly-bay raced down the trail to find the guide below awaiting him. Tossing his head with anger, he wheeled on up the trail again, and within a few yards recovered his monotonous limp and his evil expression. He was driven into camp, and there he vented his rage by kicking in the ribs of a harmless little pack horse.

His Destined End

This was bear country, and the hunters resolved to end his dangerous pranks and make him useful for once. They dared not catch him, it was not really safe to go near him, but two of the guides drove him to a distant glade where bears abounded. A thrill of pity came over me as I saw that beautiful untamable creature going away with his imitation limp.

"Ain't you coming along?" called the guide.

"No, I don't want to see him die," was the answer. Then as the tossing head was disappearing I called, "Say, fellows, I wish you would bring me that mane and tail when you come back!"

Fifteen minutes later a distant rifle crack was heard, and in my mind's eye I saw that proud head and those superb limbs, robbed of their sustaining indomitable spirit, falling flat and limp—to suffer the unsightly end of fleshy things. Poor Coaly-bay; he would not bear the yoke. Rebellious to the end, he had fought against the fate of all his kind. It seemed to me the spirit of an eagle or a wolf it was that dwelt behind those full bright eyes that ordered all his wayward life.

I tried to put the tragic finish out of mind, and had not long to battle with the thought; not even one short hour, for the men came back.

Down the long trail to the west they had driven him; there was no chance for him to turn aside. He must go on, and the men behind felt safe in that.

Farther away from his old home on the Bitterroot River he had gone each time he journeyed. And now he had passed the high divide and was keeping the narrow trail that leads to the valley of bears and on to Salmon River, and still away to the open wild Columbian Plains, limping sadly as though he knew. His glossy hide flashed back the golden sunlight, still richer than it fell, and the men behind followed like hangmen in the death train of a nobleman condemned—down the narrow trail till it opened into a little beaver meadow, with rank, rich grass, a lovely mountain stream and winding bear paths up and down the waterside.

"Guess this'll do," said the older man. "Well, here goes for a sure death or a clean miss," said the other confidently, and, waiting till the limper was out in the middle of the meadow, he gave a short, sharp whistle. Instantly Coaly-bay was alert. He swung and faced his tormentors, his noble head erect, his nostrils flaring; a picture of horse beauty—yes, of horse perfection.

The rifle was leveled, the very brain its mark, just on the cross line of the eyes and ears, that meant sure, sudden, painless death.

The rifle cracked. The great horse wheeled and dashed away. It was sudden death or miss—and the marksman missed.

Away went the wild horse at his famous best, not for his eastern home, but down the unknown western trail, away and away; the pine woods hid him from the view, and left behind was the rifleman vainly trying to force the empty cartridge from his gun.

Down that trail with an inborn certainty he went, and on through the pines, then leaped a great bog, and splashed an hour later through the limpid Clearwater and on, responsive to some unknown guide that subtly called him from the farther west. And so he went till the dwindling pines gave place to scrubby cedars and these in turn were mixed with sage, and onward still, till the faraway flat plains of Salmon River were about him, and ever on, tireless as it seemed, he went, and crossed the canyon of the mighty Snake, and up again to the high wild plains where the wire fence still is not, and on, beyond the Buffalo Hump, till moving specks on the far horizon caught his eager eyes, and coming on and near, they moved and rushed aside to wheel and face about. He lifted up his voice and called to them, the long shrill neigh of his kindred when they bugled to each other on the far plain; and back their answer came. This way and that they wheeled and sped and caracoled, and

Coaly-bay drew nearer, called and gave the countersigns his kindred know, till this they were assured—he was their kind, he was of the wild free blood that man had never tamed. And when the night came down on the purpling plain his place was in the herd as one who after many a long hard journey in the dark had found his home.

There you may see him yet, for still his strength endures, and his beauty is not less. The riders tell me they have seen him many times. He is swift and strong among the swift ones, but it is that flowing mane and tail that mark him chiefly from afar.

There on the wild free plains of sage he lives; the storm wind smites his glossy coat at night and the winter snows are driven hard on him at times; the wolves are there to harry all the weak ones of the herd, and in the spring the mighty Grizzly, too, may come to claim his toll. There are no luscious pastures made by man, no grain foods; nothing but the wild hard hay, the wind and the open plains, but here at last he found the thing he craved—the one worth all the rest. Long may he roam—this is my wish, and this—that I may see him once again in all the glory of his speed with his black mane on the wind, the spur galls gone from his flanks, and in his eye, the blazing light that grew in his far off forebears' eyes as they spurned Arabian plains to leave behind the racing wild beast and the fleet gazelle—yes, too, the driving sandstorm that overwhelmed the rest, but strove in vain on the dusty wake of the Desert's highest born.

Free at last.

Bibliography

"The King of Currumpaw: A Wolf Story"
  Scribner's Magazine 16 (November, 1894) 618-28
  and *Wild Animals I Have Known*, 1898, Charles
  Scribner's Sons

"The Pacing Mustang"
  Wild Animals I Have Known, 1898, Charles
  Scribner's Sons

"Johnny Bear"
  Scribner's Magazine 28 (December, 1900) 658-71
  and *Lives of the Hunted*, 1901, Charles Scribner's
  Sons

"Tito, The Story of the Coyote that Learned How"
  Scribner's Magazine, Part I & II, 28 (August &
  September, 1900) 131-45, 316-25 and *Lives of the
  Hunted*, 1901, Charles Scribner's Sons

"Badlands Billy, The Wolf that Won"
  Animal Heroes, 1905, Charles Scribner's Sons

"Monarch, the Grizzly"

> *Ladies Home Journal*, Part 1, 2, & 3, 21 (February, March, & April, 1904) 5-6, 47, 13-14, 15-16, 60 and *Monarch, The Big Bear of Tallac*, 1904, Charles Scribner's Sons

"Coaly-Bay, The Outlaw Horse"

> *Collier's* 56 (January 22, 1916) 10-11 and *Wild Animal Ways*, 1916, Doubleday

CPSIA information can be obtained
at www.ICGtesting.com
Printed in the USA
LVHW092207081120
671112LV00037B/262